Ainsley's list of what NOT to do the next time she sees sexy Luke Collier...

1. Don't dissolve into a drooling puddle of lust the first time your eyes meet. *(Try to show some restraint, girl!)*

2. Don't let him kiss you. *(You won't want to stop.)*

3. Don't be tempted to steal a peek when he's skinny dipping. *(You know you'll only end up joining him.)*

4. Don't tell him your secrets. *(Especially one BIG secret.)*

5. Don't give in to the overwhelming chemistry between you. *(Ha! Easier said than done.)*

6. Don't think of what might have been. *(Or of what could possibly be again, if only the stubborn, sexy man would cooperate.)*

7. Don't give him your heart. *(Right. Been there, done that. Then again, it might be too late...)*

Blaze™

Dear Reader,

Is there a hot guy from the past you still think about? The one who made you quiver from head to toe? Maybe you even imagine what life would have been like if things had worked out.

I love playing the what-if game—especially with my characters. And in *What Might Have Been* I really mess with them.

Ainsley and Luke think they're over each other. Not! As the heat between them rages, they can't help but wonder what the future holds. But when Luke learns the secret Ainsley's been keeping, all bets are off!

I hope you enjoy reading Ainsley and Luke's journey. I'd love to hear what you think of their story! You can contact me at kira@kirasinclair.com or visit me at www.KiraSinclair.com.

Best wishes,

Kira

Kira Sinclair

WHAT MIGHT HAVE BEEN

TORONTO NEW YORK LONDON
AMSTERDAM PARIS SYDNEY HAMBURG
STOCKHOLM ATHENS TOKYO MILAN MADRID
PRAGUE WARSAW BUDAPEST AUCKLAND

Recycling programs
for this product may
not exist in your area.

ISBN-13: 978-0-373-79609-0

WHAT MIGHT HAVE BEEN

Copyright © 2011 by Kira Bazzel

www.eHarlequin.com

Printed in U.S.A.

ABOUT THE AUTHOR

When not working as an office manager for a project management firm or juggling plot lines, Kira spends her time on a small farm in north Alabama with her wonderful husband, two amazing daughters and a menagerie of animals. It's amazing to see how this self-proclaimed city girl has (or has not, depending on who you ask) adapted to country life. Kira enjoys hearing from her readers at www.KiraSinclair.com. Or stop by www.writingplayground.blogspot.com and join in the fight to stop the acquisition of an alpaca.

Books by Kira Sinclair

HARLEQUIN BLAZE
415—WHISPERS IN THE DARK
469—AFTERBURN
588—CAUGHT OFF GUARD

To get the inside scoop on Harlequin Blaze and its talented writers, be sure to check out blazeauthors.com.

Don't miss any of our special offers. Write to us at the following address for information on our newest releases.

Harlequin Reader Service
U.S.: 3010 Walden Ave., P.O. Box 1325, Buffalo, NY 14269
Canadian: P.O. Box 609, Fort Erie, Ont. L2A 5X3

I want to dedicate this book to my own grandma, Mary Driscoll. I wish I could have spent more time with you over the years, but even from a distance your strength, faith and love have influenced me in only the best way. Thank you for being part of my life!

I also want to thank Al and Mary Pearson from Pearson Farm in Fort Valley, Georgia. They were amazingly kind and helpful with their information concerning peach farming. If you have a chance to visit them, please do! Their website is www.pearsonfarm.com. Any mistakes concerning peaches, farming or anything else are solely my own.

1

"THE PRODIGAL SON RETURNS," Ainsley Rutherford whispered acidly under her breath.

She looked out of the kitchen window to the long gravel drive that wound its way from the road to the small Georgia farmhouse in the middle of Collier Orchards. She could see the tail of dust kicked up by the red Jag barreling toward them.

Only Luke Collier would drive that fast over gravel. Who cared if he ripped apart the undercarriage of his expensive car by hitting one of the potholes dotting the drive? As long as she'd known him, the man had been in a hurry. And to hell with the consequences.

Shaking her head, Ainsley turned her back and walked to the kitchen table. A well-worn teapot and a plate of homemade cookies sat between two waiting place settings.

Afternoon tea was a relaxing ritual that Luke's grandmother had always followed. When Ainsley had come to stay at the orchard almost eight years ago, she'd joined in Gran's habit. There was something soothing about keeping this part of their daily routine, if nothing else, constant right now.

"He's here, Gran." The older woman—Ainsley had never been certain just how old Gran was—looked up from her chipped china cup with a serene smile on her face.

Ainsley fought the unexpected and overwhelming urge to cry. Gran's smile was so far from the grief she'd expected, the sorrow she was personally feeling at the loss of Gran's husband of sixty-five years. Pops had passed just two days before, the reason for Luke's headlong race down the drive. In the time she'd been at Collier Orchards—first as a scared and pregnant girl, then as their reluctant granddaughter-in-law and finally as the manager for the orchard when Logan had died and no one else was left to take on the responsibilities—Gran and Pops had both come to mean so much to her.

"Who, dear?"

"Luke."

"Well, of course he is." Gran went back to staring into the delicate china she held, rolling the cup back and forth in a mindless way that just wasn't like the Gran she'd always known.

A car door slammed outside. Then the soft tread of leather against the worn boards of the wraparound porch tied knots deep in Ainsley's stomach.

For the first time since he'd left, she was going to see the man who'd broken her heart.

She'd always known this day would come. But, no

matter how much she'd tried to prepare herself, there was no way to anticipate all she would feel when she saw Luke.

He'd shattered her world when he'd ended their four-year relationship. Young and blindsided by his desertion, she'd had no warning that he was unhappy. She'd been building a picture of their ideal life at the same time as he'd been planning an escape…from her and from the future this orchard represented.

At first she'd argued with him, trying to understand. But it had soon become obvious that Luke's drive for adventure, fame and fortune meant more to him than she ever had. She'd been devastated.

With one decision, he'd set into motion a series of events that had irrevocably changed her life. It hardly mattered that he hadn't realized the chaos he'd left behind.

The front door opened and closed. Luke's footsteps, heavy on the century-old flooring, clicked down the hallway toward the kitchen. Ainsley had played this moment out in her mind so many times. On random days, during empty nights. Sometimes she was angry and railed at him with her fists and words. Sometimes he begged for forgiveness and asked for a second chance. The worst were the scenarios where he didn't care at all. Where he acted as if she'd never mattered.

She knew those were closest to the truth.

Her breath lodged in her throat, a block of solid air she couldn't swallow past. And then he was there, framed by the nicked edges of the kitchen door frame.

He was larger than life. But then, he always had been. Even as she'd spent hours dreaming of a simple, safe and happy life, he'd spun tales of wealth and adventure and conquering the world. She'd envied him that. The confidence he'd had in himself and in his inevitable success.

And of course, he'd been right. He was now owner of a multimillion-dollar software company.

While he still looked much the same, there were some changes to his appearance. He was older, certainly, but then they both were.

He was harder. Not just in his body but in his face. Gone was the carefree look of mischief that had perpetually lurked deep in his eyes. Gone was the dreamer with a plan and a vision for his future.

Now he was rock solid. A businessman with responsibilities and focus. Even here, miles from anything resembling a boardroom, he stood before her in a suit that flowed over the contours of his body as if it'd been molded just for him.

If she'd needed any one piece of concrete evidence that he no longer belonged here, that expensive charcoal-gray suit would have done it. Although, he never really had belonged.

He had a few lines etched into the corners of his eyes now, but the same sharp cheekbones ripped across his lean face. A gift from some long-forgotten Indian ancestor, they matched the dark complexion that made it appear he'd spent hours in the sun when she knew he much preferred to lock himself inside a room and tinker with computers. Or, at least, he had. She assumed that piece of him would never change.

His hair, on the dark side of brown, was too long, brushing the lower edge of his collar and hanging down into his eyes. It had always been that way. Luke had no time for the mundane things like getting a haircut. Or leaving a forwarding address for his family and friends.

No one had known where he was for months after he'd left. If they had, it might have changed everything.

Ainsley had often wondered why he'd felt the need to cut ties with everyone. She knew why he hadn't told her where he was going, but she'd never understood why he'd distanced himself from Logan, his twin brother, as well.

"Gran."

Luke's voice was rough as he bent over his grandmother's shoulder, placing a kiss on her paper-thin cheek.

"Luke." The other woman reached up with a single hand and wrapped it around his neck, holding him close to her. Her knuckles turned white with the force of her grip.

That strength shocked Ainsley. She hadn't seen that much effort from Gran in a very long time.

And then Luke turned his eyes on her. Green. Vibrant. The most shocking shade she'd ever seen. It had been years since she'd seen that color…years since she'd looked into the twin of those eyes as her husband, Logan, had died in her arms on the side of the road.

Years since she'd felt the mixture of guilt, anger and undeniable awareness. Her own scars twinged, unwanted memories in her belly and leg.

When had it all gotten so complicated? When had her memory of the two brothers become so tangled together?

Luke, the brother she'd loved with all of her heart. The brother she'd envisioned a life with. The brother who had taken her love and with both hands thrown it back in her face.

Logan, the twin who'd rescued her when her abusive father kicked her out and she'd had nowhere else to go. The brother who had loved her enough to give her everything despite knowing she could never love him in return.

"Ainsley." The single word was pleasant enough. Was it her imagination that infused his voice with a host of emotions—longing, guilt, relief, anger, grief, concern?

Probably. That would be giving the man more emotional credit than he deserved. He'd never cared one iota for her—or anyone else as far as she could tell—and he was hardly likely to start today.

"Luke."

He pinned her for several seconds with his gaze. Her vanity made her wonder what he saw even as her brain told her that his opinion no longer mattered.

With a small tilt to his lips that was far from a smile, he brushed past her to take the seat beside his grandmother. Reaching across the table, Luke grasped Gran's hand. "I'm sorry I wasn't here."

Ainsley choked back a protest. Two weeks ago she'd left a message with his office about his grandfather's rapidly deteriorating health. If he'd wanted to be here he could have been.

Instead of calling him on the statement—it wouldn't have accomplished anything and would have upset Gran—Ainsley reached for a cookie and stuffed it into her mouth.

Silence settled around them, heavy and unhappy. A minute stretched to ten. Luke said nothing. Instead, he watched her. The weight of his stare and an uncomfortable awareness crawled up her spine.

Why did it bother her?

She couldn't take any more. As she pushed back from the table, her chair scraped against the wooden floor, the noise more discordant in the silence than it should have been.

With a hand to her arm, Gran stopped her. "Would you mind cleaning up, dear? I'm so tired. I think I'll go and rest."

Immediately, she felt petty. Gran was the one suffering right now and Ainsley was the one trying to run away. "Of course."

With a half smile of thanks, Gran disappeared into the hallway.

"Should she be going up on her own?"

His voice almost made her jump. She hadn't forgotten he was there—her awareness of him wouldn't let her—she just hadn't expected him to speak.

"She's fine. Do you think I'd let her go if she wasn't?"

Ainsley tried not to let the resentment she was harboring leak into her words. Who was he to ask that question now, as if he'd been the one watching her strength and health deteriorate?

Ainsley gathered the dirty dishes and turned toward the sink. Running the water to scalding, she breathed in the smell of lemon and waited for the soap she'd added to turn into a pile of bubbles. Her shoulders began to relax as she looked out the window toward the rows of trees in the distance. They always gave her a sense of peace and belonging. She'd never found that anywhere else. Certainly not in her own cold and demanding childhood home run by her fanatically religious father.

That peace was shattered when Luke brushed against her as he set the last few empty dishes on the counter.

When his body touched hers, she wanted to scream and melt at the same time. It was so wrong that one accidental touch was all it took for her senses to recognize him. To remember.

Her relationship with Logan hadn't been physical so it had been a long time since she'd felt this flush of awareness and remembrance. The anticipation and desire. It had been eight years since a man had touched her...since this man had touched her.

In all that time she'd never wanted anyone else.

She shouldn't want Luke now but apparently her body hadn't gotten that message.

The difference was she was no longer a starry-eyed, naive girl. Now she was a woman and perfectly capable of thinking with something other than her hormones.

Taking a deep breath, Ainsley pushed down her physical response and patently ignored the ache rippling through her body. She dunked a cup into the suds and rubbed vigorously before running it through the stream of water and laying it on the drain.

Luke reached into a drawer and pulled out a towel, then stepped up beside her to dry. Part of her resented that he knew precisely where everything was, even after so many years.

Gritting her teeth, Ainsley pushed that emotion down, too.

"Do you think we can get through this?"

Her head jerked around at his words, taking in the long length of his neck as he stared out the window.

Unable to watch him, she returned her focus to the sink. "The funeral? Yes. Gran seems to be handling things well. Your grandfather's passing wasn't a surprise. I think, from what she's said, they had plenty of time to say their goodbyes."

"No. I mean us. You and me. Can we get through this without tearing each other apart?"

Ainsley finished washing the saucer that was in her hand, then rubbed her wet palms on the legs of her shorts and took a step away.

Looking up into his face, she felt her throat go dry. How could she want to both rip this man's clothes off and just plain want to rip into him? To hurt him the same way he'd hurt her.

"That implies there's unfinished business between us, Luke. There's nothing to fight about, nothing to be angry about, nothing left to say or do. What happened between us is done. We've both moved on and are happy."

Swallowing the lump that was stuck somewhere between her throat and her lungs, she turned around and walked away.

Just as he'd done.

Unfortunately, before she could get far enough she heard the single whispered word behind her.

"Liar."

And she knew it was true. There was so much left to say, but she wouldn't say it. Because saying it wouldn't change anything. It wouldn't erase the past. Wouldn't bring his brother back. Wouldn't save the life of their dead child, the son he knew nothing about.

Speaking the words wouldn't take away her guilt for never telling him the truth. At first, she hadn't been able to. And then it hadn't mattered. What good could come from telling him that he'd had a beautiful, perfect son who'd lived only a handful of minutes before his little, undeveloped lungs had given out?

None.

So for now, she'd be a liar. Better that than someone who shattered his life the way hers had been shattered.

She couldn't do that to someone else.

Not even Luke.

2

LUKE WATCHED HER WALK AWAY, debating whether he should go after her. The decision was made for him when the loud and insistent chirp of his BlackBerry sounded at his hip.

With a sigh, he pulled it out of the holster at his waistband and leaned back against the counter.

"Collier."

"Luke, it's Mike. I'm sorry to bother you now but we heard back from Miyazaki Technology. They've countered our offer."

Could this day get any worse? Without even asking, he knew the news wasn't good. He could tell by his VP's tone of voice.

Exhaustion set in, bone-deep. He'd just spent the better part of twenty-four hours traveling from a small province in Japan. All he wanted right now was to fall into the nearest bed and sleep for twelve straight hours. The thought of getting his brain to function fast enough to deal with the information Mike was about to give him just made the exhaustion worse.

He'd expected a little back-and-forth negotiation with Miyazaki. That was the nature of business. He'd just planned on handling the specifics in person, which would have given him a better power position.

He probably should have been here two weeks ago, when Ainsley had called his office about his grandfather, but he'd hoped to close this deal—one he'd been working on for a year and a half—before coming here. If he was completely honest with himself, there was also a part of him that hadn't wanted to face losing yet another person in his life.

Once the deal with Miyazaki went through his plate would be clear for the foreseeable future and he would be able to focus on his grandmother and dealing with the orchard.

He'd hoped Pops would hold in there a little longer. Unfortunately, life doesn't always work out the way we want it to. Luke felt his eyes involuntarily sweep over the spot where Ainsley had stood moments before.

Shaking his head, he pulled his attention back to where it should be.

"Give it to me."

"Are you sure? I mean—"

"Quit stalling, Mike. I can tell it isn't good. Just tell me."

"They're almost five million below where we wanted."

"Son of a bitch." Luke squeezed his eyes shut, rubbing

his fingers across the bridge of his nose to combat the headache that had just ratcheted up to skull-splitting.

He was prepared to negotiate, but this was insulting.

"Put together a response, drop our price by five percent, email it over and I'll take a look as soon as I've had five consecutive hours of sleep."

And some pain meds. "Anything else?"

"As a matter of fact, someone from Brooks Farms called."

Luke waited. "And…"

"Apparently they want to talk to you about buying the orchard."

That hadn't taken long. Although he wasn't entirely surprised. News traveled fast in the small network of commercial growers. And Collier Orchards was prime, proven land. It was no secret that he'd never wanted any part of this life and most people probably assumed he'd sell as quickly as possible.

Those assumptions would be correct. He had a business that needed his undivided attention. Despite growing up here, he knew nothing about running the orchard and had no reason to learn.

"Great. Have Emily contact them with a request for an offer. And while she's at it, ask her to contact several of the surrounding farms and see if anyone else would be interested in purchasing." With any luck he'd start a bidding war over the valuable property. It wasn't often that thousands of acres of prime peach land went on the market. Apparently, he was going to need the money to make up for the millions he was about to lose to Miyazaki.

"Done. Oh, and Margaret asked about arrangements. Several of the employees would like to send condolences."

"I'll be in touch as soon as I know something."

Which gave him the perfect excuse to find Ainsley again.

Business handled, he hung up with Mike, but instead of moving continued to lean against the counter, letting his eyes roam around the familiar room. He wasn't sure what he'd expected to find but the sensation of homecoming was surprising.

So was his reaction to Ainsley.

He shouldn't want her. Not anymore.

She was Logan's widow. And while he and his twin brother had shared a lot…somehow the idea of reclaiming his sister-in-law felt wrong.

Apparently, his body hadn't gotten that memo. From the moment he'd walked in the door he'd been aware of her. Her scent, her quiet grace, the soft and understated way she seemed to fill the room.

Every movement of her body, sigh of her breath, quirk of her lips had registered in a way he honestly hadn't wanted them to.

Aside from the fact that she was now off-limits, her wholesale betrayal eight years ago should have been enough to keep him away. Sure, he'd broken off their relationship—reluctantly, knowing they could never be happy together, that they wanted different things—but she'd immediately found someone to replace him.

His twin brother.

In fact, from the time he'd heard about the wedding—just months after he left—he'd wondered if they'd been sneaking around behind his back the entire time. The thought had been gut-wrenching. The two people he'd trusted most in the world had betrayed him in the worst possible way.

He wasn't sure which had hurt worse, Logan or Ainsley.

And yet, the moment he'd seen her it had been like the first time....

Her hair, long dark curls flowing past her shoulders, had been blowing in the hot summer breeze as she'd slipped in and out of the line of trees. Moonlight had filtered down, making her seem like an apparition. It had been late, the July heat pressing down on his chest and making sleep almost impossible. He'd gone out looking for what little relief he could find in the wind through the trees. As much as he'd always resented being in this place, the whisper of the leaves on the air had soothed him in a way nothing else could.

But that night he hadn't found relief. Instead, he'd found the woman of his dreams laughing as she ran. Little white shorts and a tank top that left her stomach bare enhanced the feeling that she was part of the moon and not part of his world.

Until she'd stopped suddenly and turned.

And smiled. The most radiant, bliss-filled expression he'd ever seen.

She'd been seventeen. He'd been eighteen and getting ready to leave to start the rest of his life.

Ainsley had changed all that. Instead of cutting his ties with the orchard, for the next several years he'd returned home every chance he could to see her. Those precious stolen moments had been tough to come by.

Her father, a Baptist minister, worked hard to keep his daughter under his influence and definitely hadn't approved of him. Her mother, unable to take her father's strict views and fundamentalist ways, had left the family when Ainsley was five. Both Luke and Ainsley had been upset when her father wouldn't let her leave to follow him to school, prolonging their separation. Rather, her father had insisted on two years at the community college nearby so he could dictate her classes, her curfew and her friends.

It was difficult for them to find time to see each other. Their days and weeks together were sporadic and not nearly enough to satisfy him. But finally, the long wait had ended and she'd joined him at college.

Things were supposed to be perfect. And yet, they weren't. He'd slowly realized that they wanted different things from life. Ainsley had visions of returning to the small town she'd always known and raising a family.

The kind of life that made his chest tighten with claustrophobic dread. He'd wanted adventure and risk and reward. She'd wanted safety and comfort and constancy.

Knowing her the way he did, he understood what drove her to need those things—the instability and harshness of her childhood. She'd dealt with both emotional and physical abuse at her father's hands—the beatings had stopped when he, Logan and Pops had confronted the man, but there was nothing they could do to p[...] from the lash of her father's tongue. In the end, Lu[...] known that he couldn't give Ainsley what she wanted a[...]d he couldn't ask her to give up the security she craved to risk the kind of future he intended to build.

And he'd been right. The first few years had been rough. He'd poured everything—every cent, every waking hour, and hell, most of the hours he should have been sleeping, too—into the business and the dream he was building. He'd had nothing left over to give to another person.

In any case, it certainly hadn't taken Ainsley long to find what she'd really been looking for. In Logan.

Even as the anger and pain had ripped through him when he heard the news, he'd known that Logan was the better choice for her. He was the one who could offer Ainsley the life she'd wanted. The happiness she'd deserved.

Knowing that hadn't erased the feeling of betrayal he'd been unable to ignore, though.

Luke sighed and shook his head. There was no use rehashing the past. Not now. Although, he supposed it was inevitable for his mind to turn there given the current situation.

For eight years, he'd dreaded this moment when he'd be tied to the one place he'd never wanted to own. From the time he was ten and his grandfather had begun showing him the land and telling him that as the oldest—born minutes before his brother—it would one day be his, he'd known he hadn't wanted it. But Pops hadn't listened.

At first he'd thought breaking ties with the family would force his grandfather to give the land to Logan instead. His brother had wanted the job. And for a while he'd thought he'd succeeded.

Until Logan had been killed in the car accident. And then it had no longer mattered. Collier Orchards was destined to be his.

But not for long. He'd make sure of that. His grandfather had to have known precisely what would happen when he left the orchard to him. Luke had made it perfectly clear that he'd never wanted the responsibility of running the place, of upholding the family's expectations and traditions. He'd wanted something new, something different, something wholly his own. Which was why he felt no remorse for selling.

He did feel a twinge about moving his grandmother from the home she'd known for most of her life but there was no help for it. Besides, his money would buy her the best care possible. He'd move her closer to Atlanta and be able to spend more time with her. That couldn't be a bad thing. He was the only family she had left…and she his. They should be close. And he had responsibilities—a business to run and employees who counted on him for their living. He couldn't simply abandon them all. The needs of the many outweighed the desires of the few.

Things would work out. Pushing away from the counter, he left the kitchen. In the meantime, he needed to get organized. Switching into business mode was as easy for Luke as breathing. Even as he walked through the quiet house, looking into vacant rooms left and right, he was making a mental list of the tasks he needed to perform.

Speak to the funeral home and church. Arrange the service and burial. Find a commercial real estate agent. Talk to Ainsley about staying until the sale was final.

That was the one he dreaded, so the first task he'd tackle.

He found her at the very back of the house, tucked into a room that was no bigger than the closet in his Atlanta penthouse.

The space was cluttered. Papers were piled on the desk, and an old computer that made his heart weep a little hummed there, as well. A stack of crates sat in the corner. He wasn't sure he even wanted to know their purpose. Around the utter chaos that appeared to reign, the walls were a warm oak panel and a stream of sunshine fell through the single window and seemed to light the place from within. The room might be small but somehow it glowed.

In the middle of it all was Ainsley, her head bent over an open ledger. He could see the neat march of numbers across the columns of the page, not enough to actually read them but enough to realize that she had an efficient and meticulous hand with the books. That they weren't on the computer in front of her made him cringe. He just couldn't understand how a business, in this era of technical achievement, could still be operating in the Stone Age.

She squinted down at the page, a frown marring her forehead and twisting the corners of her lips.

He leaned against the door frame, not wanting to disturb her. If he was honest, part of him just wanted to watch her without the pressure of knowing his scrutiny was returned.

"Stop scowling."

Or maybe not.

"I'm not scowling."

"Yes, you are. And hovering, too. What do you want?"

Pushing away from the door, Luke ventured into the room and realized too late there was no place for him to go. No chair—not even buried under the piles of stuff around him. In fact, there was little vacant space on the floor except for the open pathway leading to the desk and the beat-up black chair she sat in. Stopping next to the desk, he felt as if he were towering over her. In business, he'd learned the importance of intimidation tactics, how the appearance of power could be just as beneficial as actually holding that position.

Somehow it felt wrong to be here now, looking down on her.

Picking up a pile at the corner of the desk, he glanced at it halfheartedly before putting it on top of another set of folders.

Her jaw tightened as she said, "I had that there for a reason."

Narrowing his eyes, he gave her the smallest grin and shrugged.

"We need to talk about the arrangements. I assume

Pops will be buried in the family cemetery but I don't know what church the service will be at."

Reaching out for the stack of papers he'd just moved, she banged them on the desk to realign them and then set them on top of yet another pile to her right.

"Everything's already taken care of. I've spoken to Mr. Brown at the funeral home. We were just waiting for your arrival to set the dates. Viewing is tomorrow afternoon with the burial and service on Friday."

She finally looked at him. Not the sideways glances she'd been giving him since he'd sat down and invaded her space but a full-on stare that set the acid in his stomach to roiling. He didn't like the expression in her eyes, yet he couldn't look away.

"With any luck you can be home by Friday night." *And out of my life* was left unspoken but hung between them anyway.

"Actually, I expect I'll be here for a couple weeks, at least. Until I can get everything in order to sell. I might have to come back and forth until it's all final but—"

"So you're selling." Something about the inevitability in her tone of voice bothered him. It was the logical choice. Of course she'd have expected it. Right?

"Obviously. I can't stay here, Ainsley."

"Of course not. You've moved heaven and earth not to be tied to this place. Why would anything change that now?"

Ainsley turned to stare once more at the book open in front of her, hiding her face and her eyes from him.

"I wanted to ask…what are your plans?"

"Plans?"

"After I sell the farm. I mean you've been here for a long time. I just didn't know…" His words trailed off. He wasn't exactly sure how to finish the statement his brain had started without thinking.

Ainsley laughed, a broken, scraping sound that was so unlike the pleasant tinkle of laughter he remembered that it seemed to burrow beneath his skin and itch. Relentless and uncomfortable, like chiggers.

"It's a little late for you to start worrying about me now, Luke. I'll be fine."

"It's not that…" Again, he let his words trail off, realizing that this time they'd come out completely wrong. He hadn't meant them the way she was sure to take them. Of course he had worried about her. Not that she'd want to hear that. "I just didn't know when you were planning on leaving. I was hoping I could convince you to stay on until after the sale."

He could see the emotions swirling behind her light blue eyes as she finally turned toward him again, a jumbled mess he couldn't decipher.

"I'll pay you, of course. More than enough to make up for any inconvenience."

And then suddenly fury leaped away from the rest, filling her eyes with a glowing blue flame. Scraping back her chair, Ainsley snapped the ledger closed on the desk and walked around him. All the while her eyes burned, eating away at him inch by inch.

At the doorway she turned, one hand resting on the jamb. His eyes were drawn there by the subtle glitter of a ring in the splash of sunlight. He recognized the ring immediately. His mother's wedding ring, the family heirloom his father had given her.

The fact that it was on her right hand instead of her left meant little. He knew where it had come from. Logan. And all over again he was reminded of a past he'd much rather forget.

And then her voice, low and sad pulled his attention back to her face.

Gone was the anger from moments before, replaced with a disappointment that was even worse. Anger he could deal with. Anger he could understand and recognize as an emotion he fought off and on himself in her presence. But he couldn't understand the disappointment, because she was everything he'd always known she would be when they'd been young and in love. Beautiful. Elegant. Confident. Sexy. Perfect.

Yet somehow, he wasn't what she'd wanted. Or expected.

But then, he never had been, had he?

"When did you become such an asshole?"

Her question rocked him back on his heels, almost literally. So unlike her. Maybe she wasn't exactly what he'd imagined, after all.

Before he could respond she was gone.

AINSLEY WAS SO MAD. With him and with herself for the awareness she didn't want and couldn't seem to shake. Even as the emotion rolled through her body she realized her reaction was off. She was responding to something above and beyond what Luke had said and was about to do.

But that was only part of it. Some of the anger was real and deserved. How could he uproot his grandmother from the life she'd always known? How could he ignore the memory of his family—his father, mother and brother—who were all buried on the hill overlooking the house? How could he simply walk away from everything?

How could he not feel a tie to the people who had mattered in his life? It bothered her. And she realized even as the reactions settled in that she was partly projecting her own emotions onto him. She'd have moved heaven and earth to have the kind of family he'd grown up with, people who'd loved him and supported him unconditionally…even as he'd disappointed them.

She'd never had that and couldn't understand how he could just throw it all away.

She wasn't surprised. Not if she was entirely honest with herself. Hell, he'd done it once before. Twice if she admitted that some small corner of her mind had hoped when he'd returned for his brother's funeral eight years ago he might have stayed. For her. He hadn't.

He hadn't even come to the hospital to visit her. Weak from her own injuries and the loss of the baby, she hadn't been allowed to attend Logan's funeral.

Some part of her had always been grateful that at least Luke had returned for that one day. Even if he hadn't cared enough to stay.

But that didn't mean she couldn't be angry with him now for doing what was best for him and not what was best for his grandmother. It was exactly what she'd expect from him…but still, it was disappointing.

Logan had done so much—taking her in, offering her a family and a future when everything had seemed so bleak. In her heart, she'd known she was taking advantage of his generosity and love. But she hadn't had anyone else to turn to.

Abandoned by Luke. Disowned and discarded by her own father. Sick and threatened with losing her child if she didn't go on total bed rest. Without a home, a job, or a way to support herself she would have ended up losing the baby.

On her worst days after the accident, she'd wondered if that would have been better. She'd lost Alexander anyway. And Logan, as well. In the end, he'd paid for her mistakes with his life.

It was a terrible repayment for the help he'd given her.

Marrying her, he'd given her a home, a family, much-needed health insurance and the support of someone who'd cared for her.

If she'd often felt bad about not being able to return his love…she'd told herself it would come in time. And maybe it would have, if they'd had a chance.

But she doubted it. Every time she'd looked at Logan, she'd seen Luke instead. She'd been a coward, but what else could she have done?

She'd been honest with Logan. He'd always known. It was the only thing that made the guilt ease even a little. She'd made her choices, but then so had he.

She had to admit that part of her felt some small measure of relief at the thought of leaving this place. Yes, she loved it. With every last fiber of her being. It had become for her the happy, bright, loving home that she'd never had growing up. No one here had ever disapproved of her, berated her, belittled her intelligence or her choices. She'd blossomed here at Collier Orchards, finding her own inner strength and purpose in life.

But there was a part of her that felt life had simply been on hold for the past eight years. She'd stayed here out of obligation and affection for Gran and Pops, knowing that she was all they had. Logan had given her so much; she couldn't abandon his family when they needed her.

Despite his heart and drive, Pops had been too worn-out to carry on with the day-to-day operations of the orchard. For a while Logan had done that. When he was gone Ainsley had taken over.

Now the world was open to her. She'd dreamed of going back to college, finishing the degree she'd abandoned upon finding out she was pregnant. She even had applications sitting on the desk in the office. She'd submitted a couple of long shots, and had meant to fill out the others so many times. But money, time and location were all obstacles she hadn't been able to overcome.

Now she could take the chance.

She could start a new life for herself and maybe forget the loss in this one.

She didn't have much. She'd saved a little money over

the years. She had no problems working. She'd find her way. And this time she'd do it on her own.

Because she could.

As long as she didn't commit murder first. A few days, a couple weeks at the most. Surely, she could survive living in the house with Luke for that long.

The memory of him standing in the doorway to the office flashed across her mind.

He was tall and lean. There was an edge to him that hadn't been there the last time she'd seen him. Hard. Lonely. And yet, she knew the softness of the dreamer he'd once been. She wondered if it was still there, beneath the polished stone surface or if the no-holds-barred world of corporate America had beaten it out of him.

Why did she care?

Unfortunately, he still intrigued her. She didn't want him to. And yet, she couldn't seem to keep her eyes off him. The moment he entered a room she was aware of him in a way that she'd never experienced with anyone else.

It was disconcerting, and she'd expected more from herself.

Her resolve would have to be stronger.

But he'd shown zero interest in her since he'd walked in the door. Well, aside from wanting to make sure she'd stay on until he sold the place.

And that didn't bother her at all. The fact that he'd thrown money in her face did. He'd assumed it would take more than her affection for Gran and common human decency to keep her here. She wondered whether his assumption said something about him or her.

What really bothered her, though, was that while he'd sat on the desk, his tight, suit-clad thigh practically shoved in her face, she'd been trying desperately to ignore her yawning and stretching libido. And he'd been giving her sidelong glances, not to look at her cleavage, but to eyeball the open accounts ledger.

It was humiliating that she could feel this way. Still. Over Luke.

3

LUKE STARED AT THE CRACKED ceiling. His head was pillowed on his folded arms, a single sheet draped across his naked body to the waist.

For about three seconds he'd felt weird sleeping nude with his grandmother two doors down. But this was what he preferred and with summer beginning to set in, he'd quickly remembered how bad the insulation in this old house really was. The ancient and inadequate air conditioner simply couldn't keep up with the creeping heat.

Despite the fact that he was jet-lagged beyond belief, he couldn't sleep. Certainly the temperature wasn't helping, but it was really the woman next door that was frying his brain. Each and every time he closed his eyes, memories of the past surfaced. The darkening of her eyes with passion. The breathy sound she made when she came. He'd wondered if she'd still do that.

And then he'd wondered if his brother had heard the same sound.

He'd spent the past hour vacillating between pounding arousal and rushing resentment.

And here he'd thought he'd come to terms with the situation years ago. Not as if he could do anything about it now. The past was done and his brother was dead. End of story.

But something in him said it was unfinished. They were unfinished.

He heard the creak of the floorboards outside his door. The soft and slow tread of feet against worn wood.

He knew who it was. There were only two other people in this house and Gran wasn't strong enough to walk with that quiet grace.

Maybe that's why he was here. Now. So they could finish this. So that he could truly move on.

The moan of a stair galvanized him and before he realized what he was doing he was out of bed.

He pulled on a pair of worn jeans he'd draped across the footboard, not bothering to do up the snap as he slipped into the hallway.

A single light burned from the kitchen, illuminating the stairs and the house below in a weak, watered-down light. He couldn't see her but he could hear the slap of the front door as it closed.

Curiosity and the remnants of a desire he didn't want had him following her.

As he watched, she slipped into the orchard at the edge of the deep green lawn. Even here, peach trees, the reason for their existence were always just steps away from the front door, a reminder of the pressure of who and what he was.

A flash of the memory he'd had earlier in the day returned, overlaying the past with the present in a way that left him shaken and a bit disoriented.

This time she didn't run through the trees with happiness and abandon. Instead, she trailed her hand slowly across one trunk, the pull of the bark almost holding on to her hand, unwilling to let it go, until she was reaching for another. As if she was unable to continue walking if she wasn't touching at least one. She moved, dreamlike from tree to tree, weaving in and out of them in a figure-eight pattern that played peekaboo with his line of sight.

Time seemed to unravel, the years and the hurt and the guilt and the anger melting away as she ghosted down the path ahead of him.

He could go back again and start over. The question was, would he do things differently?

He didn't know.

For some reason he was drawn to watch her in silence, staying back several yards, moving in and out of the shadows himself to stay hidden. There was something about her, about the tilt of her shoulders and her heavy footsteps that held him back.

She didn't want company, certainly not his, and he had no idea what to say to her anyway. There'd been a time he would have understood immediately what she was thinking, what she needed. Not anymore.

Part of him missed the feeling of knowing someone almost as well as he knew himself. He'd shared it with

Logan, until they'd begun to grow apart. He'd shared it with Ainsley.

She stopped in the middle of the orchard, her hand resting lightly against the rough trunk of the tree. She looked up through the canopy above, reaching on tiptoe to pull a round orb of fruit from a limb.

He expected her to rub the dirt from it and take a huge bite. He remembered the immediate burst of juice and fruit in his mouth when he'd eaten a ripe peach straight from the tree as a child. He could almost feel the cool roll of the juices down the back of his throat, sweet and sticky on his fingers.

His own mouth began to water. But she didn't eat it. Instead, she wrapped it tight in the center of her two hands, rubbing it back and forth across her palms as if to caress the soft downy skin.

The gesture was almost absent, probably something she'd done more times than she could count.

He could see the gentle rise and fall of her chest on a sigh as she stared at the dark patch of star-studded sky. After a few moments, she slipped her hand into her pocket and left the fruit there. It was a round bulge at the outside of her thigh.

She walked through to the west of the property. It took him a few minutes to realize what her destination was. He was shocked when he finally did.

The family graveyard lay this way, about halfway back.

In typical fashion, the small square of land was surrounded by a low-slung, black wrought-iron fence. There was a small gate, big enough only for one person to pass through at a time.

The space was beginning to get crowded; he could see the march of headstones, worn and moss-covered in the back and new and shiny in the front.

His family history. He should probably feel something, standing on the edges of so much history. He didn't. Or rather, he did for his brother, whose stone would be one of the newest. He'd never actually seen it, though, as he'd left before it was placed. He didn't feel anything—not curiosity, connection or obligation—for the ones further back. For the people he'd never known.

Even his parents, who'd died when he and Logan were three, were distant memories of people who'd hardly shaped his life.

Perhaps in a few days, when Pops disappeared into the ground, he'd feel more.

At the moment, what interested him was Ainsley.

Instead of going inside as he'd expected—to visit Logan, he supposed—she stopped to the far right of the fence. Leaning her back against a tree, she let it take her weight, her body almost bowing over itself.

He wondered what she was doing here, staring out across the lonely space, until the clouds shifted across the moon and a shaft of light filtered down over her face.

Then he realized she was crying.

Silent and alone.

SHE HADN'T MEANT TO COME HERE. It had been the last place she'd wanted to visit tonight—her emotions, jumbled up and complicated as they were, too close to the surface. But she'd been drawn here, almost against her will.

Maybe it was Luke. It was inevitable that she'd think of Alexander with him so close. And Logan, of course.

Her son and husband were both buried inside the fence in front of her. She couldn't seem to make herself enter. Not tonight.

It had taken her months to visit the first time. Months for her to forgive herself, God, Luke and the world for what had happened to her son. Months for her to realize tragedy happened.

Seeing Luke brought some of it back.

What she had missed, what she had needed, in those first few lonely days had been someone to hold her and tell her it would be all right. It might have been a lie but that hadn't mattered.

But no one had been here. It had taken her a while to finally work up the strength to tell herself what she'd needed to hear. She'd found an inner strength she hadn't known she possessed.

However, when the nightmares came as they had tonight, the visions of the crash and the hazy memories of sharp, searing pain and loss, sometimes she still wanted someone to hold her and tell her it would be okay. She wanted what she'd had with Luke before it had all gone so wrong.

She was finally ready to move on, to find that kind of kinship and connection with another human being. To share her soul and her life with someone else.

In a few weeks she'd be able to do just that. To put the past behind her and move forward.

Maybe that's what her nightmares and the tears tonight were for. A goodbye.

Inside her pocket, her fingers worried the flesh of the peach that she'd plucked. She'd planned on eating it when she'd first reached up and then at the last minute couldn't do it. Memories of picking fruit from these same trees with Luke, of him licking the juice from her chin, lips and fingers, had stolen the joy from the moment.

It was almost as if her body had been lying dormant all these years, waiting for him to return and spark her pilot light.

She resented it.

And yet, she'd take it as a sign that her life was finally starting up again, as well.

Tears rolled down her face, plopping quietly onto the ground at her feet. She cried for what they'd had, what they'd lost and the future they'd never had the opportunity to explore.

She was alone and she let them go. Better here, now, surrounded only by the orchard, than later with Gran. Or Luke.

At least she thought she was alone, until his arms came around her.

She knew immediately that it was him. Her body responded in the primitive way only he seemed to force from her.

Even as her shoulders strained toward him, she pulled her spine away.

"What are you doing?"

"Holding you."

"I didn't ask you to."

"You didn't have to."

His strength was more than she could fight. Giving in, Ainsley let herself go slack in his arms. Their bodies collided, shoulders to chest, breasts to abs, knees to thigh. She let him take her weight, her arms lax at her sides.

His heat enveloped her, warmth surrounding her. It should have been uncomfortable in the oppressive air. It wasn't.

Twisting her head, she laid her cheek on the swell of his chest. She realized her tears had stopped almost as suddenly as they'd started.

His chin rested on the crown of her head. She could feel the brush of his lips against the strands of her hair. She shouldn't be able to feel such a minute sensation, but somehow everything the man did registered in her brain. On her body.

She sucked in a heavy breath. He smelled of the night. Dark. Different. More wild in a way, and yet somehow still the same.

"Tell me why you're crying."

"No."

"Why not?"

"It's private."

He paused and shifted against her.

"There was a time when you could tell me anything."

"There was a time when I didn't have to. You already knew. That time is gone."

She began to push back, leaning more heavily into the tree behind her.

And yet, he wouldn't let her go. Instead, he followed her, this time pressing his body into hers instead of the other way around.

His hold had changed, gone from comforting to wanting in the space of a few breaths. She could feel it in the tension of his muscles, the edge of leashed anticipation that coursed beneath the surface of his skin.

The same sensation surfed through her own blood now.

He reached down and wiped a single finger across the blade of her cheekbone. It came away wet with the traces of her tears.

At his touch, a shiver rocked her from her scalp to the soles of her feet, leaving lightning licking across her skin.

He didn't wait for her response; instead, he leaned in and placed his lips on the point his finger had just traced, at the edge of her hairline.

His breath was warm on her face. She could smell the bitter dregs of coffee and the sweet tinge of sugar. He'd taken a cup upstairs with him after dinner.

She sucked in a breath as the tip of his tongue darted out to trail the smallest line across her cheekbone and straight to her lips.

She could taste the salt of her tears on his tongue as he followed the line of her closed lips.

She couldn't help it. She opened for him, gasping in anticipation and denial.

He moved immediately, taking more than she'd ever thought to offer. In one fleeting moment his kiss went from gentle and soothing to hard and demanding.

His hands wrapped around the nape of her neck, bowing her up and bringing her closer to his body. She could feel all of him. The powerful, lean muscles beneath his skin. The strength he hid behind his corporate facade. The proof of his desire, long and hard between them.

He fused his mouth to hers, pushing in and taking whatever he wanted. And she was powerless to stop him. Not because she lacked the strength to pull away. Not because he would have kept her there if she hadn't wanted him to. But because she couldn't find the will to douse the fire he'd ignited deep inside her belly.

A fire that had been nonexistent for far too long.

His teeth nipped at the edge of her bottom lip, sucking it deep into his mouth. Then he let it go, trailing the heat of his kisses down the curve of her exposed neck.

She whimpered. His mouth felt so good, starting a burning ache at the center of her sex.

Her head rolled back against the tree trunk and her eyes popped open as his teeth grazed the pulse pounding at the edge of her collarbone.

And her gaze landed squarely on Alexander's grave. The small white stone with the single carved angel.

This time her sharp intake of breath had nothing to do with desire and everything to do with self-disgust. What was wrong with her?

This man had been the catalyst for every bad moment in her life. He'd abandoned her just when she had needed him most. He'd turned his back on everything they'd shared, on the life they could have had together. Six hours in his presence and she was panting for more.

Slapping her hands to his chest, she scrabbled for enough purchase to push him away.

Immediately, he stepped back.

They were both breathing hard. His eyes, the color of a new spring leaf, glittered at her in the moonlight. She could see the heat in them, knew the same desire smoldered in her own.

She held up her hands and took a few steps back from him and from her own body's betrayal.

The sting of tears threatened again as she spun away and melted into the dancing leaves around them.

The last thing she needed to be doing was kissing Luke Collier in the shadows beneath the peach trees as if none of their past had ever happened. As if he wasn't about to take away the one true home she'd ever had. As if she didn't have secrets to hide.

As if they still cared for each other.

She'd meant nothing to him then and she meant nothing to him now. The problem was that Luke Collier had been the love of her life. And up until this moment she'd thought that was past tense. But the force of one brief kiss had proved to her that if she let herself, she could fall for him all over again.

And get her heart crushed for a second time.

4

"LET'S START OVER."

Luke walked into the kitchen the next morning armed with resolve. Somewhere between lust and the realization that it wasn't going anywhere he'd found clarity.

As long as he and Ainsley both breathed he'd want her.

He could live with that. At least for a few weeks.

What he couldn't live with was the potential for her to disappear on him when he needed her most. He didn't think she was the kind of woman to leave him high and dry simply for retaliation's sake, but he wasn't taking the chance. As she'd pointed out last night, he no longer knew what kind of woman she was.

"What?"

He could see from her startled expression and the flashing rise of a flush to her skin that she hadn't heard him coming. Considering the floors creaked as if they were about to buckle under at any moment, that was saying a lot. He wondered briefly what had held her attention, then decided it was none of his business.

"We…got off on the wrong track last night." And that was an understatement if ever he'd heard one. That kiss had been so far out in left field. "Listen. I'm sorry. I shouldn't have kissed you. Let's just chalk it up to the past tugging at my heartstrings."

"I didn't think you had a heart, let alone strings."

The flush on her skin rose higher and she rolled her lips in on themselves as if she wished to pull the words back. And as much as he'd like to pretend they hadn't hurt, they had. However, showing her that wouldn't get them anywhere but right back to square one…full of emotions neither of them wanted or needed.

Shaking his head, Luke continued. "I know you don't necessarily agree with what I'm doing, but I honestly think it's the best course of action. I can't stay here, Ainsley, and I can't ask you to." There was too much history for that. It was hard enough knowing that she'd been here, in his family home, all these years. Putting her on the payroll just seemed wrong. "I know you have plans and I'm not asking you to change them too terribly much. Just stay long enough to help me transition. Please."

Begging grated against his nerves, but he'd learned long ago that ego had no place in business. And that's what this was. Business. Nothing more.

She stared at him for several moments. He watched as her teeth worried the inside of her cheek, her lips pursing and contracting.

Finally, she opened her mouth to say, "You mentioned money."

And he knew he had her.

"Absolutely. I assume you've been drawing a salary from the orchard. I'll double it if you stay until the final papers are signed. However long that takes."

"You don't even know how much that is."

"Doesn't matter."

This time it was her turn to shake her head. "You're either very stupid or very cunning."

On solid ground for the first time since he'd followed her into the orchard last night, he let a smile—of triumph and self-satisfaction—through.

"Let me know when you figure it out."

A twinkle entered her eyes and he could have sworn that the corners of her lips twitched.

"On one condition."

"Name it."

Crossing her arms over her chest, Ainsley narrowed her eyes and straightened her spine. He could tell she was ready to play hardball, ready to make a stand. He'd seen the signs often enough on the other side of the negotiation table. He was intrigued and wondered what, exactly, she felt so strongly about.

"You can't just leave everything to me. While you're here—and since you're hell-bent on selling off pieces of your heritage—you're gonna see exactly what you're giving up. Learn what it takes to run a place like this."

Luke's muscles jumped beneath the calm facade he'd adopted. She'd surprised him. He'd expected her stand to be more personal, selfish even. Instead, she was concerned for him. For what he was giving up.

Not that it made any difference. It was just interesting.

"I already know what it takes to run this place. That's why I'm selling."

"I find that hard to believe. You were a boy when you left and your grandfather took care of the details. You have no idea what he, and every one of your ancestors, put into this orchard. I think you should at least know the value of what you're throwing away."

"I have every intention of knowing the value…we're going over the financials today."

"There's more to the world than money, Luke."

"Yeah. There's technology and progress, two things that this place seems allergic to."

Shaking her head, Ainsley dropped her arms to her sides and a wistful expression crossed her face. "Whatever. My one requirement."

It was no more than he'd planned to do anyway. He wouldn't dream of entering into negotiations for an asset he didn't fully comprehend the value of. The best way to do that was to get his hands dirty. He'd learned that lesson early on, his hands deep into the guts of computers for hours on end.

He might not like it, but he'd do it.

However, she didn't need to know that. "All right," he said, the words ringing with reluctance.

Turning to flip the switch on the light above the sink, she tossed a towel onto the counter and headed for the doorway. Stopping even with his shoulders, she turned her head and looked at him.

"And just so you know, I would have stayed for nothing. Do you really think I would have left Gran alone with you?"

With a final sweep of her gaze down his body, she bounced on her heels and headed out the door.

Her scent brushed past him, a combination of lemon, peach and warm summer. He wondered if she'd already been outside this morning and thought she probably had. Farm life equaled early-morning chores. Already he could hear the insistent whine of machinery in the distance. He had no doubt that if he went outside he'd see people handpicking the trees. When the hottest part of the day was miserable, it paid to start your work at first light.

He stood there, rooted to the floor, clenching his fingers into fists. The urge to reach out for Ainsley as she'd stood beside him had been strong. Stronger than he'd expected.

Last night he'd convinced himself that nostalgia and the dreamlike quality of the moonlight had helped to tear away the barriers between them. That without the otherworldly film transforming the moment, he never would have touched her. Never would have been overwhelmed by the urge to kiss her.

Apparently, he'd been lying to himself. Today there was nothing but early-morning sunlight and the clear, crisp scent of a clean kitchen between them and he felt the same urges.

The difference was this morning he'd kept himself in check. And he'd continue to do that for the foreseeable future.

From the hallway he heard the musical lilt of Ainsley's voice as she taunted, "Are you coming? Some of us can't afford to stare at the kitchen wall all day."

Well that truce didn't last long, he thought ruefully following her.

SHE SHOULD PROBABLY LET UP on the taunting. Teasing a tiger was dangerous.... But right now, it was the only surefire way she knew to keep him at a distance. Hopefully he'd be so distracted by her sniping, that he wouldn't notice the weakness she felt toward him.

Her standoffish attitude was also a reminder to herself that their past was far from rosy and glowing. As much as she shouldn't, apparently, she needed that reminder.

The problem was, the heat still lingered between them. And she didn't like it.

Ainsley walked into the office and sat down at the desk. She wasn't surprised when Luke showed up seconds later; she'd all but dared him to follow. Perhaps she should have thought through the taunt before she'd lobbed it. In reality, she would have much preferred a few moments alone in order to get her wayward thoughts and libido back under control. Again.

"So. What are we doing?"

"*We* aren't doing anything. I'm going to get in touch with an agency about hiring more workers to pick the fruit when it's ready. I'm expecting we'll be ramping up the harvest in the next week or two."

"Haven't we already started?"

Ainsley shook her head. "We're late this year."

Mother Nature and the fruit dictated when to harvest, as much as their commercial clients would have preferred otherwise.

"We have a standing contract that we need to fill. I'm sure you'll want to take a look at it, as it'll be part of any sale."

Spinning around in her chair, Ainsley began digging through a drawer for the paperwork. She took delight in the bemused expression on Luke's face when she plopped the lengthy document down next to his hand.

Not that she didn't think he was more than capable of handling it, Mr. Multimillion-Dollar International Corporation. But there was no denying he was out of his element when it came to the vagaries of farming contracts.

Reaching over, he snatched up the sheaf of papers and started thumbing through. Just like yesterday, he crowded into her space. Not that there was much of it to be had in the tiny room... He filled the area around her, his hips propped against the edge of her desk, his long legs stretched out before him, blocking her escape route. The overwhelming and heady scent of him surrounded her.

Turning away, she pulled in a deep breath, hoping it would be devoid of him. It wasn't.

The blood beneath her skin felt as if it was strumming

faster, a primitive beat that was relentless and unavoidable. "It's up for renewal at the end of the season?"

"Sure."

"Why aren't we locked into a longer contract? You said we've been dealing with this company for years."

"You never know what might happen. The trees get disease, or they stop producing. Or someone decides to sell. Besides, it goes both ways. While the relationship has been profitable for us for a very long time, the short contract allowed us to keep our options open, as well."

His only response was a noncommittal grunt that made her want to smack at him.

"Remind me, this help you're hiring...how long will they be here?"

"As long as it takes."

"And is this the only time we hire migrant workers?"

"You know the answer to that, Luke."

He looked up from the document he was still scanning, a frown on his face. "I'd rather not rely on my memory after all these years, especially since I paid as little attention as possible," he said. "Pretend I don't know anything about peaches." Then he returned his focus to the papers in his hand.

Part of her resented his ability to read while carrying on a conversation with her. It had taken her hours the first time she'd read that damn contract. Hours with a Google page open so she could search for the legal terms she didn't understand.

"I assume they're still migrant."

"Yes." Ainsley shrugged. It was a facet of their business. They didn't need full-time employees to maintain the trees. They hired seasonal workers several times throughout the year, whenever they were needed. Collier Orchards maintained a regular staff of five or six who managed all the off-season work. They would never have made a profit if they'd kept workers on the payroll who had no job to do most of the year. And they treated all of their employees very well, while they were there.

"I suppose I should wait until after the harvest to sell," he mused.

She didn't think he expected an answer but she gave it to him anyway.

"Well, that depends."

"On what?"

"On who you sell to. Any of the neighboring farms would simply take over the management of our orchards and fulfill the contract themselves. Someone outside of the area might have problems." She paused, surprised at what she was about to say but she couldn't stop herself.

"I'm surprised that it even matters, though. Why are you worrying about something that could be someone else's problem?"

Dropping the contract back onto the desk, he crossed his arms over his chest and looked at her. Really looked. She wasn't expecting the impact of his gaze and her stomach did a barrel roll to her toes.

With a half smile tugging at his lips, he said, "Money."

She should have known.

"What gets me the best price? Do I get more from the

sale of the property if the buyer has a contract in hand and a guaranteed buyer for the crop? Or do I make more by fulfilling the obligation ourselves before closing the sale? Options. Options are always a good thing. They put you in the power position."

Oh, he knew everything there was about the power position. He'd always maintained it in their relationship. While she, she'd been reduced to doing whatever she had to in order to survive.

She just shook her head, unwilling to say something she might regret. At some point if not right now.

"Let's take a walk."

AINSLEY TRAILED AHEAD OF HIM, spouting a lengthy monologue about things he didn't care to know about.

Around them a sense of frenzy permeated the atmosphere. A large group of people scattered between the trees worked tirelessly, picking the fruit from the branches by hand.

His BlackBerry buzzed at his hip. Dragging his attention from the woman in front of him, he glanced down at the screen and realized it was Mike. Without putting a stop to her monologue, he answered the call.

"Collier."

He ignored Ainsley's glare as he listened to his VP on the other end of the line.

"Luke, do you have access to a fax machine? I just emailed you the counteroffer and need it signed and back to me as soon as possible so it can be waiting for Miyazaki when they open."

Luke's mind turned with the logistics of handling the problem. From the middle of nowhere. He carried a portable printer for his laptop…with as much traveling as he did he'd learned quickly not to rely on anyone else's technology. He eyed Ainsley's stiff back as she continued to walk ahead of him. Based on the lack of modern technology he'd seen before, he'd bet there wasn't even an ancient fax machine buried somewhere in her office—the kind that still used rolled thermal paper you could only buy from mom-and-pop office supply stores.

He'd find a fax machine in town. "Yeah. Give me a couple hours and I'll have it back to you. Good work, Mike. Thanks for handling this for me."

Without waiting for a reply, he disconnected the phone. They walked along in silence for several minutes before he decided an apology might not be a bad idea.

Increasing his strides, he ate up the ground until he was standing beside her. Wrapping his hand around her arm, he pulled her to a stop until they were facing each other. The space between them was too big and too small all at once. Part of him wanted to let her go and part of him wanted to pull her closer.

"I'm sorry. I had to take that. Please. Continue."

She refused to look him in the eye but he could see her glare as she raked him from head to toe beneath the cover of her dark lashes.

"Honestly, I wouldn't have taken that if it hadn't been important."

She sighed, but continued anyway. Extricating her arm, she turned back to the path, picking up where she'd left off, explaining that each tree would be picked multiple times during the season to ensure that the peaches were perfect when they came off the branch. There was a finesse to handling the harvest. Peaches were funny things; they could be underripe one day, perfect the next and spoiled the following day. If each tree wasn't picked regularly they could lose a substantial amount of crop... and money.

She was telling him things he already knew, but he'd asked her to think of him as someone with no prior knowledge. He had purposely distanced himself from the farm growing up. While some of the information had filtered in just from proximity, he had no way of knowing what was important and what wasn't.

He studied the people around him, clearly hot and covered with the sweat of their labor. It didn't look fun to him at all.

Ainsley ran her hand over the trunk of a tree, telling him all the dangers they had to watch out for. All the things that could sink the entire orchard in the blink of an eye.

Precisely the risk he'd wanted nothing to do with.

If he'd made this his life's work he'd have always worried when it would end. When it, too, would be taken from him by some catastrophe. Farming was not for the faint of heart.

He understood, better than most, how easily he could lose the things he cared about.

He'd known that from the time he was three.

And everything he'd learned since then had reinforced his fears.

He'd lost his parents, his brother…Ainsley.

She stopped by a tree. They were acres into the orchard, the gently waving leaves above them.

She reached up, just as she'd done last night. This time she strained more, going on tiptoe and leaning hard into the trunk for leverage.

"Here. Let me."

He came up behind her, saw the fruit just out of her reach and lifted to his own toes to grab it.

It was a moment before he realized that she'd stiffened beneath him.

And when he stopped, he realized why. His chest was pressed tight to her shoulders. The arch of her spine curved away from his body but that only seemed to emphasize the round curve of her rear as it pushed into his thighs.

His response was immediate. And damn hard to miss, especially pressed into the downward arch of her spine. Clearing his throat, he stepped away, bringing the peach she'd been reaching for with him.

She moved, too, sidestepping to put more space between them. The skin in the deep V of her T-shirt was flushed, drawing his eye to the skittering pulse at the side of her neck. She licked her lips and looked away.

Part of him wanted to see her eyes. They'd never been able to lie to him. He'd have known immediately what her response to him was.

Part of him knew that if he saw the slightest interest

there, he wouldn't be able to stop himself from a repeat of last night.

The difference was that it was broad daylight and they were surrounded by people. They might both be able to lie to themselves and pretend that moonlight and nostalgia had been responsible for last night's kiss. But if they did it again now, the smoke screen would be gone. And, frankly, he needed that smoke screen if he wanted to survive the next few weeks with his sanity intact.

Thinking about last night, though, brought up a question he'd wanted to ask…and had been too distracted to think of it before.

"I saw you pick a peach last night."

She darted a glance at him from the corner of her eye and answered, "Uh-huh."

"Why didn't you eat it?"

To his surprise the skin across her neck and shoulders turned an even brighter shade of pink. Not exactly the response he'd expected.

"Um, wasn't ready."

"Then why'd you pick it? I don't believe that you didn't know that right away."

She shrugged and looked at him. "I wanted to feel it in my hands."

The same way he wanted to feel her in his hands? He knew that wasn't what she'd meant but couldn't stop the thought.

"There's something about it that's settling. Knowing that trees have stood on this land, produced the same fruit over and over again, for a hundred years. That's longevity. That's stability."

That's what she valued most in this world and always had. Even as a teenager just starting her adult life, she'd wanted something safe and stable. Something her father had never provided.

Luke fought a twinge of regret and guilt. He'd left her precisely because he knew he couldn't give her the one thing she'd always wanted. And here he was taking it away from her now that she'd found it.

But he couldn't let that sway him. He was doing the right thing, making the right decision. Not just for himself but for everyone.

She'd find what she was looking for in another place. With another man.

For some reason, that suddenly bothered him very much.

5

LUKE HAD NO IDEA WHERE Ainsley was headed until they rounded a corner in the path to stare at a building he did not remember. It sat next to the packing facility he *did* remember and was about half the size of a normal barn, not huge but not exactly small, either.

When she walked up to the large double doors that fronted the structure and rolled them back, he thought he'd died and gone to heaven. Inside were several machines. Some he didn't recognize, but clearly visible in the front were two four-wheelers.

He and Logan had spent years begging his grandfather for something they could tear through the few areas of vacant land on. He'd flat-out refused. Always said they were expensive, unnecessary and dangerous to boot.

"How'd you manage this?"

Luke walked over to the nearest one and ran his hand across the red paint. They were clearly used, beat-up and scratched all over. But he'd bet they flew across open ground. And would spin up mud like you wouldn't believe.

"Logan didn't tell your grandfather. He just came home with that one." She nodded to the one his hand currently rested on. "Pops came around eventually. Especially when he realized that without them he couldn't make it to the back forty by himself."

"He certainly did hate to be dependent on anyone else, didn't he?"

Ainsley smiled, a wistful expression that made him sad even as it melted away.

"You know how to operate one of these?"

"My Harley could beat this thing any day, but I'm sure it'll do in a pinch."

As his machine roared to life, he was surprised to see Ainsley shoot out ahead of him onto the path leading back into the grove. Hell-bent for leather, her hair a streaming flag for him to catch.

The delicate tinkle of her laughter ghosted back to him as he opened the throttle and followed suit. Man, he'd love to see the expression on her face, eyes alight with mischief and happiness, a monster-size smile tugging at her lips, and her cheeks pink from the bite of the wind whipping past.

She stood up on the pegs, leaning over the bars as he drew closer.

These were the kind of memories he'd wanted to make with Logan.

And like that, his brother stood between him and Ainsley once more. He pulled back, but it was several moments before she realized that he'd slowed the four-wheeler.

Plopping back into the cradle of the seat, she nodded her head to the right and took a sharp turn beneath the trees.

Reducing their speed and staying in the cleared spaces beneath the peach trees allowed them to pass through the rough terrain.

Once again, it took him several minutes before he realized her destination. The pond. He'd almost forgotten it was out here.

As he and Logan had grown up, they would slip out to the pond in order to talk and simply be alone. To escape the sadness that sometimes seemed to permeate the old farmhouse. While he and his brother had lost their parents, it had been a long time before he'd realized that his grandparents had also lost their son. Wrapped up in his own grief he hadn't appreciated theirs. He supposed it was normal for a young child to be so self-absorbed.

As he'd gotten older, he'd understood more.

He, Logan and Pops had spent many spring and summer days at the pond, fishing poles in their hands. He couldn't remember ever catching anything; he wondered if that was because the pond wasn't actually stocked. Or whether he and his rambunctious twin had inadvertently chased all the potential dinners away.

Ainsley turned the four-wheeler as they approached, killing the engine and letting the machine come to rest at the end of the dock built out over the still water.

He did the same, slowly dismounting and walking onto the sunbaked, dark-stained wood.

It creaked quietly beneath him, welcoming him back.

A memory flashed into his mind. Logan had been dozing beneath a tree, exhausted from the crash of a sugar high—Pops had given them Coke, cookies and a bunch of candy and sworn them to secrecy.

But Luke had refused to leave his post by the poles.

He'd sat cross-legged on the dock, his line bobbing gently in the water, his back tucked in tight to the four-by-four post at his back.

His grandfather had sat opposite him, his worn fishing hat drooping into his eyes and shielding his face from the sun.

Luke had thought Pops was dozing, as well, until he spoke.

He'd been…ten at the time, he supposed.

"Your grandmother and I are proud of you, son."

His grandfather's praise, along with the sunshine beating down, warmed Luke from the inside out.

"You're doing well in school and you look out for your brother. But it's time for you to start helping around the farm more. All this will be yours one day. Your responsibility."

Like that the warmth faded away. Even at ten he knew he didn't want the responsibility. He didn't want to be tied to the uncertainty of farm life. He'd seen the struggle his grandfather had gone through in the lean years, barely scraping by. That kind of life wasn't for him.

"I don't want to run the farm, Pops."

Pops flipped the brim of his hat out of his way and speared Luke with his gaze. "I won't live forever, Luke. You're the oldest. Collier Orchards will be yours." His words trailed off but Luke could hear his final mutter, "Always passes to the oldest."

A nasty knot curled in the pit of his stomach. The thought of Pops dying, like his parents, left the bitter taste of helplessness in his mouth. Pops and Gran were his family. He couldn't think of losing them, too.

He'd known one day it would happen. Pops wasn't exactly young. But not now. Not yet.

In an effort to block the churning thoughts, Luke focused on another part of his grandfather's speech.

Responsibility. Tradition. He was sick of it. Sick of being constantly reminded of the ancestors who had sacrificed and worked hard to keep this land going. He didn't want their land. He wanted something of his own.

He wanted out of this sleepy little town. Out of the oppressive summer heat and wishy-washy winters.

"No. I'm not staying here, Pops. I don't want the farm."

Throwing his pole down onto the scarred surface of the dock, Luke pushed past his grandfather. He sprinted into the trees, ignoring the hollers coming from behind him.

It was the first time he'd openly defied his grandfather. It wasn't the last over the final rocky and volatile years they'd spent together. They'd loved each other—they'd both known that. But they'd wanted different things for Luke's life.

So why did that suddenly make him feel guilty?

"How can you turn your back on all this?"

He looked over and saw Ainsley, her head thrown back, her eyes closed and a serene smile gently turning her lips. Sunlight streamed across her body, as if it had been sent only for her.

Her legs, long and lean beneath a pair of shorts, seemed to glow. He hadn't realized how tanned she was until just now, but considering the hours she spent outside it made sense. A flowing tank top did little to hide her body. In fact, it did everything to accentuate the curves beneath.

When he'd left she had been a girl. Now there was no mistaking that Ainsley Rutherford was a woman.

Luke took an involuntary step toward her. He could envision the moment. Her gasp of surprise as he tugged her to him. Her eyes flying wide as he kissed her again…

He couldn't go down this road a second time. Being with Ainsley again was a fantasy that could never happen. Not when she'd married his brother.

Pulling up short, Luke was thankful that she had no idea he'd taken a step toward her. He didn't want to know what her reaction would have been…welcome or rebuff.

He closed his own eyes for a moment, calling on the memory of the one thing that could stand between them. The one person who could remind him why this was so wrong.

"You never talk about him."

Ainsley's eyes flew open as she jerked around to look at him. "Who?"

"Logan. You never talk about him."

A frown crashed over her face, pulling her cheeks in and making her face seem longer, harder. "What do you want me to say?"

He shrugged. There was no safe topic that involved Ainsley and his brother. He didn't want to know about their life together. And yet, he did. It was like picking at a scab even knowing that it was going to bleed and hurt once you ripped it off.

The temptation was just too much to ignore.

"I haven't once heard you talk about his death. Your grief." Maybe that was something they could share…their grief over the loss of his brother. "How did you deal with it?"

She just looked at him, a strange light whispering deep in her eyes. "I didn't."

He stepped closer to her. This time he had a plausible reason—comforting her. Not that she seemed to need comforting. Not like she had last night.

"What do you mean?"

"I was in the hospital for weeks, Luke. I had multiple broken bones, a punctured lung and internal bleeding. I was in and out of surgery for the first few days and then so drugged up that I could barely remember my name."

The pain that stole into her eyes just about killed him. It was deep. An emotion he could identify with and understand. She must have cared more for Logan than he'd realized.

Jealousy, red-hot and rampant, melted into his blood. Shouldn't he be past this by now? Apparently not.

But even as he fought the jealousy, the thought of her suffering… It left him cold and sad. He'd had no idea.

"No one told me."

Why hadn't they? Why hadn't Gran or Pops said something? He knew Ainsley had been in the accident, as well, knew that she'd been injured, but they'd promised him she was fine. Recovering and simply too weak to come to the service.

At the time he'd figured she also hadn't wanted to see him. And he hadn't wanted to see her. Losing his twin brother was difficult enough. Seeing Ainsley would have been more than he could handle.

But my God. If she'd been in that much pain. That broken and torn apart…

"You didn't ask, did you?"

But he had.

"Yes, I did, Ainsley. I asked about you. They told me you were going to be fine. That you didn't want to see me."

GRAN SAT IN THE OLD ROCKING chair in the corner of the den. The room was rarely used now; Ainsley preferred to spend her time either in the office or the kitchen.

Besides, this room had always been Gran's. As Pops had gotten weaker, she had often found him and Gran here together. Gran quietly pushing back and forth in the rocker while she worked on whatever knitting project she'd picked up, Pops dozing on the chintz sofa. The room was open and airy, light streaming in from the floor-to-ceiling windows on the far wall.

Now it was somewhat sad to see the older woman in here alone. Sitting in silence. The needlepoint bag lying untouched at her feet.

Ainsley sat on the chair beside her and waited for her presence to be acknowledged.

When Gran finally turned to look at her, Ainsley asked, "How are you today?"

Reaching out, Gran patted the top of her hand as it rested on the arm of the chair. Her skin was paper-thin and dry and in her mind, Ainsley could almost hear the crackle as it rubbed against her own.

"I'm fine dear."

Again, they sat in silence. There just wasn't much left to say.

"Have you picked out something to wear tonight or would you like me to help?"

This time when Gran reached for her, it was to lay her hand longways against Ainsley's cheek.

"Such a sweet girl. No, I'm fine."

Ainsley nodded and secretly planned to steal upstairs and just check to make sure that what Gran had laid out actually matched. The older she got, the more eccentric her wardrobe choices became. It was probably a combination of being stuck in a fashion era of the past and having gained enough years that no one really questioned her clothing choices. Ainsley usually let her alone but for today she'd be representing the family and she knew that Gran would never want to disappoint.

"I wanted to ask you something." Something that had been bothering her ever since she and Luke had talked on the dock this morning.

"Luke said that you told him I didn't want to see him. When he came home for Logan's funeral."

Gran swiveled her head to look at her and simply nodded.

"Why?"

"Well, because that's what you told me, dear."

"No, I didn't."

"Of course you did, honey. You were in and out of it what with the pain and grief and medications but whenever you surfaced you started talking about Luke. At least, for the first few days. It took us a while to figure out what you were saying but…you didn't want him to see you. That was clear as day."

Gran's eyes suddenly sharpened to the brightness that Ainsley remembered from her first few years here at the orchard.

"You didn't want him to know about the baby. You most definitely didn't want him to know about Alexander."

Ainsley sucked back a gasp, holding it in because she didn't want Gran to see her reaction.

It was the first time the other woman had ever indicated that she'd known Alexander had been Luke's and not Logan's. Gran had never asked and she and Logan had never said.

"I… It's not…" Ainsley just stared at the other woman, panic and guilt welling up inside.

"Don't worry, I won't say anything. But I really think you should. At the time I realized it would only hurt—you and him—and there was really no reason, as it wouldn't have changed anything. But I think you should tell him now, Ainsley. I think he needs to know, don't you?"

"But—"

"It isn't good to keep secrets, dear. Especially from the people we love."

"I don't—"

Dismissing the denial she was about to utter, Gran pushed up from the rocking chair. Her movements were unsteady, the moving chair making an already difficult task even more so. But Gran refused to give up her rocker. She'd once told Ainsley that she'd spent many long nights in that chair…nursing and holding Luke's father.

It was the kind of history, the kind of loving memory that Ainsley didn't have. She couldn't imagine her father staying up all night to console her about anything, let alone rock a crying infant back to sleep. He hadn't had the patience.

Or the caring nature.

Ainsley just sat and watched Gran leave, certain any denial she might utter would sound completely false—it did in her own head. And knowing that any excuse for her behavior would sound petty and selfish—because it was.

She might have had good reasons then for what she

did...but there was certainly nothing keeping her from revealing the truth now.

Nothing but her fear that Luke would hate her and never forgive her.

Not that it mattered. When the sale was complete they'd go their separate ways and probably never see each other again.

"Second chances don't come around often, Ainsley." Gran paused and turned back to look at her. "Trust me when I say, fifty years from now you'll regret it if you throw this one away."

And then she was gone. Her words ringing in Ainsley's ears and echoing hollowly through her body.

As much as Gran might like to think so, this was not a second chance.

It was a goodbye.

6

SHE WAS SITTING IN THE KITCHEN, a cup of tea cradled between her hands. For some reason, after her conversation with Gran, she'd needed the warmth.

She hadn't bothered with the full trappings of tea, unable to eat anything even if it was bite-size or loaded with sugar.

That's where Luke found her. He startled her when he entered the room, keys dangling from his fingers.

"I'm heading into town. Do you want to come?"

She wanted the escape, more desperately than she'd realized until it was offered. But she was worried about leaving Gran and they only had three hours before they needed to be at the funeral home for the viewing.

"Gran's sleeping. I left her a note and asked Mitch to check in on her in case she wakes up before we get back. I don't expect she will, though. Come on, Ainsley. It'll do you good to get away from here for a little while."

It was precisely what she needed to hear. There was so much to be done—early summer was one of their busiest seasons. But they had excellent people working for them and Mitch, their operational manager, and his men knew what they were doing. They could survive without her for an hour or two.

Without really answering Luke, she got up from the table, set her half-filled cup into the sink and walked to the front of the house. She felt a little guilty for leaving the dirty cup there. But she knew it would wait for her. Right now she needed an escape from this place, from the weight of the loss of Pops and from the memories that Luke's presence had stirred up.

Besides, it had been weeks since she'd been to town just because. Summer was a busy time on the orchard and with Pops's illness and death...

She could hear the tread of Luke's feet behind her, heavy and close. He kept bouncing his keys in a way that made her want to whip around and snatch them from his hand.

The ride into town was uneventful. He drove fast, faster than she'd have liked but even she couldn't deny the burst of adrenaline through her body as they'd zoomed away from the house and the responsibilities waiting for her there.

While part of her fought against the panic that always came with driving fast down country roads, she could tell from the way Luke handled the wheel that he knew what he was doing.

But then, she'd thought Logan had, as well.

And he would have been fine, if they hadn't been

arguing. It was the one and only time they'd ever fought. And that day it'd been over Luke.

Over whether she should tell him about Alex. They'd only found out where Luke was a few days earlier. Until then the option had been closed to her.

Logan had wanted her to let Luke know about the baby, but she hadn't been ready to change the way she'd built up the pregnancy and raising her child in her mind. Without Luke. She wasn't prepared to let him back in. Not after he'd left her so easily.

Not then.

And after that it had no longer mattered.

Luke pulled up in front of the county courthouse. She wasn't sure why it hadn't occurred to her, but she'd never imagined this was his destination.

"I need to run inside. Do you want to come?"

She most certainly did not. Whatever he was doing most likely had to do with the sale of the orchard, and while she'd resigned herself to the inevitable, that didn't mean she'd support him on the decision.

"No. I'll pop into a couple of the stores down the street."

He just nodded and walked away.

She wandered, allowing the early-afternoon sunshine to warm her bare shoulders and the top of her head. She spent quite a bit of her time outdoors, but usually she had an agenda. Right now, she had no responsibilities, no pressures, no expectations to meet. She felt liberated and a little anxious, not quite sure what to do with herself.

There were several quaint little shops along the strip.

Old brick buildings with as much history as the farmhouse.

There were antique stores, an elegant-looking interior design firm, a photography studio and the cutest toy store she'd ever seen.

She stood outside the display window, watching the toys. There was a model train set up, complete with moving drawbridge, tiny houses and miniature trees. Off to one side, they'd even erected a peach orchard, paying homage to the area's livelihood. She stared as the train went round and round the track and was embarrassed to feel tears sting her eyes. Alex would have loved something like this.

She could just see him, seven now, bouncing up and down on his knees as he manipulated the controls of the train. In her mind she saw long, masculine legs cross the scene to rescue the overturned train from the wreck her rambunctious son had caused. And realized it wasn't Logan in the scene in her head, but Luke.

Blinking away the vision of what might have been, she was startled to see Luke standing beside her, his reflection in the window watery and weak.

Spinning around, she put her hand to her thumping chest. "You startled me."

"I'm sorry. I didn't mean to. You seemed so engrossed in watching the train."

She shook her head, swallowing the lump of tears that was lodged in her throat.

"Are you ready to go?" Luke asked.

"Absolutely."

He fell into step beside her as they headed to the car.

"What were you thinking about back there?"

As much as she wanted to outpace him, and the future they'd never have—she knew she couldn't. His legs were so much longer than hers.

"You looked so sad."

"I was thinking about…Logan."

She'd almost told him, the combination of the powerful image still lingering in her mind and Gran's words making her tongue loose.

But this wasn't the time. Or the place.

"Logan." Luke's voice was suddenly gruff. And hard in a way that made her shiver.

His face closed down, going from optimistic and happy to thoughtful and displeased in the blink of an eye.

"Did you get what you needed?" She hadn't realized until the expression was gone, but he'd certainly looked content with whatever he'd found in the courthouse.

His only response was a nod.

She slipped back into the welcoming leather seats of his car. They rode in silence again, only this time instead of being pleasant and almost comforting, it was fraught with unsaid words and accusations.

Leaning her elbow on the armrest, she propped her head on her fist and stared out the window. The scenery was as familiar to her as her own body. And yet, she didn't even really see it.

She didn't realize what he was doing until he'd pulled off onto the shoulder of the deserted country road. There was a patch of gravel, sprinkled just before the bridge across one of the local creeks. She supposed it was there for people who wanted to pull off and do a little fishing.

They were hardly here for a quick cast.

"What are you doing?"

Killing the engine and slipping the keys into his pocket—the pocket farthest from her—he said, "Tell me about Logan."

She looked at him as if he'd gone crazy and for a moment wondered if he actually had.

"About your marriage."

And in the blink of an eye she understood.

"Why?"

"Because I want to know."

"No, you don't. You want to punish me. You want to hurt yourself. Why?"

He laughed, a sound that didn't come close to making her feel warm and fuzzy. "Maybe I'm a masochist."

"Maybe you should let it go."

With a growl, he pushed open the door and jumped out. He prowled to the hood of the car, his body taut with quiet grace and barely leashed fury.

She watched him. She couldn't stop herself. There was no denying he was beautiful. It would have been like trying to convince herself the sky was green. You couldn't dispute what was in front of your face.

She crawled from the car, as well. There was something about the lonely way he stood there, hands shoved deep into his pockets, his back so straight and stiff she wanted to reach out and smooth her hand down it. Smooth the tension away.

But she didn't touch him. She didn't think either of them could take that right now.

Instead, she stood beside him, staring into the same quiet abyss as he.

Finally, after a few moments, he turned to her. While his face was blank and smooth, his eyes were a storm of turmoil. A storm she felt inside her chest, threatening to rip her apart.

It was the torture in his eyes that made her speak, made her say things to him that she'd sworn she never would.

She quietly asked, "What do you want to know?"

"Did you love him?" The words burst from him in a rush, filling the air between them.

Ainsley closed her eyes and sighed. There was no easy way to balance self-preservation against soothing his wounds. Weeks ago she never would have expected to feel the need to reassure him. To tell him that she hadn't immediately turned to his brother—the person he'd been closest to in the world—for solace when he'd gone.

But now she realized she couldn't let him remain this conflicted, this angry, with his brother.

"Not in the way you mean. He didn't replace you. He couldn't."

He glanced over his shoulder at her, a question clearly there, yet one he left unspoken.

Walking over to the rusted pipe that framed the outer

edges of the small country bridge, Ainsley leaned her elbows on top of it and searched for the right words.

"I cared about him. I never would have married him if I hadn't, no matter what…." She trailed off, half-afraid that he might pick up on the subtext swimming between what she'd actually said and what she'd left unspoken.

But apparently he didn't notice.

"He loved you."

It wasn't a question but a clear statement of fact. Something that he'd obviously known for years and years.

She answered anyway. "Yes."

"He told me. When I called. I guess a couple months after the wedding. A week or so before he died."

She nodded even though she knew he probably hadn't seen.

There was plenty of space between them. Dry, dusty dirt, the elegant lines of his empty sports car. But the physical space couldn't compare to the gulf of mistrust, misunderstanding and anger.

It didn't matter that they were talking; neither of them looked into the other's face, the other's eyes. Ainsley was afraid of what she'd see reflected back. As well as what she might inadvertently reveal. Luke had always been so good at reading her.

She wondered why Luke chose to turn away from her.

"He was angry. At me. He wouldn't tell me why, though. But I knew it had something to do with you. He told me to stay out of your life. That I'd made my choice and we'd all have to live with it. I didn't understand what he meant, then. I still don't."

But she did. Although it really didn't make much sense. Why would Logan warn Luke away one day and then try to convince her to talk to Luke?

Maybe his conscience had gotten to him. Not that he'd ever had anything to be ashamed of.

"I never knew it, but Logan loved me from the very start. He just never said anything while we were together."

Blinded by her own obsession with Luke, she'd been completely oblivious to Logan's feelings.

And then Luke had left. And she'd been in trouble. And Logan had offered her the one thing he'd wanted desperately and she'd needed so badly. Marriage.

"Look, Logan was happy if that's what you're worried about. I didn't take advantage of him."

That did get his attention. He took a single step toward her, but more than that he finally turned to face her, full on and looked into her eyes.

"I never thought you had."

She supposed that was something.

"I might not have loved him, with the kind of all-consuming passion that you and I had, but I cared for him. A great deal. I would have done anything. If I could have, I'd have switched places with him in a heartbeat. You have no idea how often I wanted it to be me in the ground instead of him." It certainly would have ended her guilt.

He took another step closer. "Don't say that. Logan wouldn't have wanted that."

"Maybe not, but that doesn't make it better. He was there for me when I had no one, Luke, when I needed someone desperately. I owe him more than you'll ever know."

He reached for her then. Gently unfurling her clenched fists from around the bridge post and turning her toward him. His arms went around her, a warm haven, the kind of support she'd rarely known in her life.

"But you didn't love him?"

Burying her head in his chest, she let his shirt gather her words. "No. And I think that makes it even worse."

They simply stood there, her heart racing between them, his chest rising and falling on labored breaths. Even now, talking about his brother—her husband—they couldn't seem to shutter their physical awareness of each other.

They both knew it was there. At one point in time those moments of electricity had been the best part of her life. What she looked forward to most out of every day. And then their connection had been gone, and all that was left was the pain of memory and the yearning for something that was no longer hers.

And now, in the charged energy between them, that recognition and need was there again. It tempted her to do things she knew she shouldn't. The longer she spent close to him, the more she couldn't remember why giving in was a bad thing.

Her body was clearly winning.

After a few moments he pulled away, resting the palm of his hands on the swell of her hips and looking her squarely in the eyes again.

"I do have one more question. If you didn't love him, why did you marry him?"

How was she supposed to answer that? She couldn't tell him the truth. Wasn't ready to tell him the truth even if she'd thought it would make a difference. Not when they were finally starting to communicate without anger and unhappiness between them.

So she settled for part of the truth, but not the most important part. Her father would have told her a lie of omission was still a sin.

He'd be right. But it was hardly her worst one.

"Because I needed someone. And you weren't here."

7

THE SHRILL SOUND OF THE phone startled Gran out of her reverie…out of the good memories that had been her companion through the pain of the past few weeks.

She sat at the table, waiting for Ainsley or Luke to pick up one of the other extensions. Oh, yes. She'd forgotten for a moment that they'd gone into town. She pushed unsteadily from the table and grasped the receiver.

Phones were so different now. She could immediately sit back down at the table, taking the cordless extension with her. Shaking her head, Gran punched the button that Ainsley had showed her would answer the call.

So many buttons these days.

"Hello?"

"Can I speak with Luke Collier please?"

"I'm sorry, he's not here." She hoped he and Ainsley got back soon, though. They needed to leave for the funeral home in a couple hours.

"Could I leave him a message?"

"Certainly. Let me find a piece of paper." Her joints

moaned in protest as she stood and walked to the far side of the kitchen. She reached into the drawer where Ainsley had arranged the few things she'd need.

"This is his Realtor. We have someone interested and they'd like to meet to discuss the property."

Gran stopped scratching as soon as the woman on the other end had said Realtor.

"Do you have a number where he can call you back?"

The woman recited it and Gran pretended to write it down.

"I'll ask him to call you."

Disconnecting the line, Gran tore the small square of paper from the pad, ripped it into several pieces and slipped them into the pocket of the fuzzy robe Ainsley had bought her last Christmas.

Before she could sit down again, Luke walked in through the open door.

"Who was that?"

She looked up at him, meeting his eyes squarely. "Someone calling about your grandfather's funeral arrangements."

With a nod, Luke retreated again. She should probably feel bad about what she'd just done. But she didn't.

Some people needed a little help to realize what was important.

THE VISITATION WAS GRUELING. Luke had stood at the front of the small chapel at Brown's Funeral Home— the only funeral home in town—with Gran on his right,

Ainsley on his left and the open casket behind them, as a steady stream of people walked through to pay their last respects.

People he'd never met, or hadn't seen in twenty years, stopped to tell him stories of his grandfather. Or stories of his parents. Or stories of his brother. Or stories of himself.

Most of those stories might have had a sentimental or humorous slant, but they'd all exhausted him. They'd brought back memories of his own and reminded him of just how much he'd really lost in his relatively short lifetime. The two hours had turned into an emotional gauntlet he hadn't expected.

The three of them had each taken a private moment with Pops before the director had closed the casket and told them everything was ready for the service the following day. As they exited the building, Luke was surprised to find that late-afternoon had given way to the watery tones of early-evening.

The heat of the day still lingered, though, and despite spending most of his days in suits, the heavy, formfitting fabric had long since become cloying and claustrophobic. At the moment what he wanted more than anything was a few minutes of freedom. From his own memories and from the ringing disappointment of everyone he'd spoken to. Because what had inevitably followed each of those touching stories was an expression of disappointment that he planned to sell the orchard and throw away his heritage.

In his head he knew the little old men and women

who'd spoken thought they were doing the right thing. In reality they were just reinforcing his decision. There was no way he could live in this place. He couldn't stand up to the expectations of the entire town…of people he barely even knew!

Hours later, their words were still ringing in his ears. Slipping on a pair of nylon running shorts, Luke headed out the door into the night, into the quiet. It was well after ten, but it had been days since he'd been able to go for a run and he figured tomorrow didn't look promising. His time would be filled with more grief and responsibility… getting a few moments to run and clear his head was hoping for too much.

He hadn't always loved to run. But he'd discovered, after an unusually stressful day at the company, that he'd needed to find some small space of clean air to breathe in the ever-pressing walls of the city. He'd strapped on tennis shoes that were at least six years old and set out. It wasn't until he'd found a small park several blocks away that the pressure in his chest had finally started to ease.

Only to be replaced by a stitch in his side about half-way around the mile-long track. He'd limped home that night and been almost unable to walk the next morning. But two days later he'd been out there again, needing the green grass, tall trees and open spaces to clear his mind.

It had become his stress relief in a world he'd piled high with stress.

Tonight he needed the same escape, the same mindless

oblivion that let the hamster on the wheel in his brain take a rest.

There was something calming about the terrain as he ran. The gentle rhythm of his feet hitting the worn paths between the trees. The rustling of the wind through the leaves above his head.

The silence.

Although it might not be the safest thing he ever did, he often ran at night because he rarely made it home before the sun was down. The park was deserted...just as the orchard was right now.

Still. Silent. And all his.

He rounded the bend and the pond came into focus. A sliver of moonlight shone on the clear surface. The only sounds that cut through the night were the occasional harrumph of a bullfrog or the whine of a cicada.

It was beautiful here. He could almost convince himself the pond was ancient, enchanted and had never been touched by human hands before tonight.

It also looked inviting, especially when he realized that his skin was sticky with sweat both from his run and the heat of the summer night.

With a quick glance around, he shucked his shorts, folded them beneath a tree and dived in.

The frogs would let him know if anyone approached.

THEY WOULD HAVE. IF SHE hadn't already been there, in the shadows.

Ainsley watched as he took a running leap off the dock, almost as if he expected the boards to spring with his step, and jackknifed cleanly into the water. There was barely a splash as he slipped beneath the smooth surface.

She knew from personal experience, not just years' worth, but having come from the water herself twenty minutes before, that the middle was deeper than it appeared.

At five foot five inches, she couldn't touch the bottom. She'd guess that Luke, at just over six feet, could probably stand on the bottom with the crown of his head just breaking the surface.

He popped up, his shoulders clearing the water before dropping back down to bob at the surface.

He whipped his head back, using nothing but gravity and motion to clear the droplets from his face. A few still clung. She watched as they glinted and rolled down into the hollow of his cheek.

She should make a sound, let him know she was there. But she didn't want to. She much preferred to watch him in silence. At first her tongue had been tied by the un-expected show of skin she'd gotten as he'd stripped to nothing. Shadow and light played across his body, high-lighting his physique. She didn't remember the dimples at the sides of his rear being quite as defined. She could probably dip the tip of her pinkie into one of them. His thighs, too, were harder than she remembered. Even from this distance, she could see their solid strength.

But the flat planes of his abs and the way his chest widened before tapering to a pleasant V at his waist… that was the same although perhaps a little more sculpted.

She hadn't gotten as good a view of that angle as she'd have liked.

And if she were honest, that was why she sat here, on the quickly hardening ground. Waiting for another, better, view of him. If she spoke up now she was afraid he'd go all modest on her.

He ducked beneath the surface again and she shifted forward, watching and waiting for him to come back. Wondering where he'd show up next. The water rippled where he'd disappeared. She strained her eyes, playing a game of hide-and-seek with him that he was unaware of.

The powerful kick of his legs brought him halfway across the pond before he surfaced…right at the edge closest to where she sat.

Here at the perimeter of the pond, the water was more shallow. When his feet hit the silt bottom, he shot up from the water again. This time the rippling surface barely lapped at the jutting edge of his hip bones. Water rolled down his torso, at first in a torrent and then slowing to tiny droplets clinging to his skin.

Her tongue burned for the right to reach over and lap them away.

Strong hands reached up, running through his hair and slicking it back from his face.

Her breath caught, a combination of fear of exposure and a need so sharp it stole her ability to think.

For a moment, when he opened his eyes again, she thought he'd seen her. But instead of recognition, shock or arousal, his gaze simply slipped past her hiding place.

She was tucked in the shelter of three trees, the shadows dark and almost impenetrable thanks to the thick canopy over her head. So why was he the one naked and she the one feeling exposed?

She wanted to see beneath the concealing ripple of the water that protected the best part of him from her gaze.

The words, the whispered request for him to come out of the water to her, clogged in her throat, victims of her inability to swallow. Before she could catch her breath he was gone again, kicking out once more for the far side of the pond.

She watched him swim back and forth, stopping briefly every five or six laps across the open space. And with each passing second the burning deep in her center leaped higher until she was a writhing mass of needs and nerves.

Finally, just when she thought she couldn't take any more, he drifted toward the dock and pulled himself up onto the worn boards.

Releasing a pent-up breath she'd been holding for who knows how long, she finally let her eyes slip shut in a prayer of thanksgiving—whether for the experience of seeing him or the thought that her torture was finally over, she wasn't sure.

She slumped against the tree closest to her, physically exhausted from the state of hyperawareness she'd been in for the past twenty minutes.

However, her relief lasted only seconds.

When she finally looked back, expecting to see Luke

putting his shorts on she was instead shocked to find him stretched out across the dock, hands pillowed behind his head, a wet stain from the water on his body spreading beneath him.

Completely naked.

And she nearly swallowed her tongue.

Yeah, she'd seen it before…a long time ago.

Had he grown? Or had her girlish memory just not realized exactly how large a man he really was?

A ray of moonlight sneaked through the branches surrounding the pond, like a stripe painted across his torso, dissecting him from one shoulder to one hip.

His knees were bent over the edge of the dock, his feet dangling into the water. He kicked gently, back and forth, almost as if the movement was a memory of the exertion he'd just expended in the water.

Her heart galloped in her chest. She honestly wondered if its pace was normal…if she could live through it moving that fast. Surely it was unnatural, her reaction to this man.

"You can come out now."

For several seconds she thought about ignoring him. He was bluffing, taking a stab in the dark based on some small sound he'd heard in the woods.

"I know you're there, Ainsley."

His words were soft, carrying on the summer breeze that blew between them. He even twisted his head, so that he looked directly at her.

He couldn't possibly see her…but it was clear that somehow he knew just where she was.

Pushing up from the ground, she bit back a groan as her muscles protested the awkward position she'd forced them into for longer than they liked.

As she stepped from the shadows, she straightened her shoulders and refused to blush at being caught spying on his midnight swim.

Walking halfway to the dock, she tried to keep her eyes on his face as she asked, "How'd you know?"

He laughed, glanced down at his perfectly hard erection and said, "Let's just say that I could feel your eyes on me."

At his words, she couldn't keep the flush from ripping up her skin. She didn't know which was worse, being caught or knowing that he'd realized she was there from almost the first moment. And hadn't stopped her.

He had no modesty. He didn't try to hide himself or his arousal from her in the least.

"We never had any problems with the physical aspects of our relationship, Ainsley. In that, at least, we were perfectly compatible."

What he left unsaid was that apparently they'd been terrible for each other in every other possible aspect of their relationship.

She couldn't help it. Her eyes slid down the length of his body. He was there for her, a feast for the eyes, and she was too close—both to him and the edge of her restraint—to deny herself.

The muscles at the center of her sex tightened with the sting of her denial, trying to convince her that what she really wanted was to cross the space between them and join him on that dock. She wanted to run her hands down the rise and fall of his muscles, feel the pull of his skin as it slipped beneath her palms, lick the pearls of water that clung to the raised pucker of his nipples.

"Come here." His words were husky, his eyes glittering beneath deceptively drowsy eyelids as her gaze finally jerked back to his face. He held a single hand out to her.

She shook her head...but took two more steps before her brain stopped the forward motion.

Even as she halted, her body strained toward him. Her breasts, free beneath the slightly damp T-shirt she'd thrown on, swayed against the material. The threads that had been soft and worn just moments ago were now torture devices for her raised and begging nipples. Even they were drawn to him and the oblivion of sexual release that she knew they'd find together.

He was right; they'd been spectacular in bed. He'd more than rocked her world, and she had no doubt that Luke could do it again. And again. And again.

If she let him.

With a groan, he dropped the outstretched arm across his eyes, shielding himself from her.

"Why are you torturing us both? Either come here, Ainsley, or go away. Your choice, but make it now before I lose what little control I have left."

She finally looked at him, not just at the overt evidence of his arousal but to the signs beneath. The tension that bowed his shoulders and hips down into the dock, the need stamped clearly in his drawn jaws and corded neck.

She'd done nothing short of look at him and his erection appeared hopeful and impatient. She wasn't the only one fighting against a need so hard it hurt.

They had that in common. And they could find relief in each other.

And at this precise moment relief felt like the most important thing in her life. From the sexual tension that had done nothing but climb since he'd walked in the front door. From the whipcord strength of the memories he'd brought with him. From the swirling emotions she wasn't strong enough to deal with right now.

And he could give that to her. She could give it back.

Reaching for the hem of her shirt, she crossed her arms, pulled it over her head in one swift motion and threw it behind her into the trees.

He must have thought the rustling sound had been her hasty retreat. With a large sigh, he released the breath he'd been holding and dropped his arm back to his side with a thud.

When his eyes finally rolled up to see her, half-naked, standing at his head, the shock hit him hard. Although it was quickly replaced with a desire so hot it almost scared her. It burned so bright, she wasn't sure she could live up to his expectations.

She'd been a rather limber and adventurous teenager when they'd been together before. Her muscles had definitely lost some of their elasticity.

And she'd carried a baby for six months and had a few stretch marks to prove it.

But he obviously couldn't see any of that. His eyes traveled down the length of her body, a caress she felt to the tips of her toes.

He surged up from the dock in one quick and graceful motion to stand before her. She expected him to reach for her, to pull her in and take over. She'd gone as far as her impetuous gesture could take her.

Instead, he stood for several seconds, his hands balled into tight fists at his sides.

And with a rush, turned away, shooting back into the water, all gleaming muscles and flashing skin.

HE SURFACED JUST IN TIME to see her running away. With a groan, he realized that she'd taken his quick plunge into the cool water completely wrong. He hadn't been trying to escape from her, but regain some measure of his control and sanity. If he'd reached for her, standing before him half-naked in the moonlight… He wasn't sure he'd be able to keep himself from tearing into her.

He'd wanted her that badly.

More than he'd ever wanted another woman in his entire life. Even Ainsley herself.

While his need for her eight years ago had been a constant ache at the center of his body, it had been nothing to the burning obsession that had almost taken over every speck of him…including his sense of reason.

All he'd wanted was to grab her, roll them both to the ground and take everything she had to offer him.

Not the best way to finesse a woman.

He could yell out. Stop her. But he didn't.

It was better this way.

Better they not start something that couldn't go anywhere and would only end up hurting them both. Again.

Better they not dredge up a past that would always loom between them.

Diving back under the water, he closed his eyes and held his breath. The currents he'd created eddied around him, holding his body suspended in the murky depths. He wasn't afraid, knowing he could reach down with his toes and push himself up from the bottom at any time.

What he needed was the solitude and loneliness of the small pond. The pressure for air burning against his lungs made him concentrate on another pain besides the ache in his groin.

The ache to have her. The ache to make her his again.

But she wasn't his. Hadn't been for a very long time.

Even as his vision grayed from pushing himself to the edge, the way she'd looked standing before him filled his mind.

Beautiful. Her skin, dusky and pale in the moonlight. Her hair, damp and disheveled from her own swim in the pond, falling over her shoulder to curl gently around her breasts. The tips of them as dark as the skin of an overripe peach. He'd bet they were as velvety and luscious, too.

As much as the vision of her had been mesmerizing

and almost more than he could handle, it was the memory of the expression in her eyes that had him groaning in a loud rumble.

Bright with passion, glittering with a need that echoed through his body even now. And just as he'd turned from her, the dismay and bewilderment had replaced the desire.

He was going to have to talk to her. To convince her that he hadn't rejected her.

Shooting up from the water, Luke was out of the pond in record time. He didn't even bother to grab his clothes, instead leaving them in a pile beside the dock as he tore off through the trees after her.

He couldn't let her go. Not like this.

8

ANGER AND RESENTMENT burned in her throat like acid. How could he turn from her that way? How? When she had swallowed her pride and offered him absolutely everything?

She knew how. He was an arrogant, sadistic SOB who delighted in cutting her to the core.

She yanked at the shirt she'd scooped up as she'd run past him and tugged it over her head even as her bare feet pounded into the dense ground beneath her. Dirt squished up through her toes and every now and then a small jab of pain shot through the soles of her feet.

She should have stopped to snag her shoes, too, but hadn't immediately seen them in the dark and hadn't wanted to wait around to look for them. Besides, the pinch of pain was fuel for her anger as she ran through the trees.

The rustling branches seemed to whisper to her, "Idiot. Idiot. Idiot."

She couldn't agree more.

What kind of moron was she? A desperate one, apparently.

She hadn't realized just how desperate until she'd turned to him. To Luke, the last person on earth she should have wanted.

Her lungs burned, against the effort and the disappointment and rejection. She inhaled a ragged breath and knew she needed to stop for a second before she collapsed.

Turning off, she went to the far side of a tree and sank onto the ground at the base of the trunk.

Ainsley hugged her knees up to her chest and pressed her forehead to them. She could feel the dampness of perspiration from her hairline as it stuck her skin together. Clammy and uncomfortable, she left her head there anyway, preferring that to facing what she'd just done.

While she could pretend to be angry with Luke, she was really more upset with herself. What had possessed her to throw herself at him like that?

Lust. Pure and simple.

What was it about that man that had her throwing away all her principles, resolve and sense of self-preservation?

With him, the promise of a few fleeting moments of pleasure overrode absolutely everything else. And it always had.

He had been her one and only act of defiance. Apparently, she was still willing to throw everything away for the chance to be in the presence of his ambition and determination. For the chance to believe that the world was just as he always saw it, ripe with possibilities and open to absolutely everything.

She knew better.

Life was a string of disappointments and grief relieved by whatever contentment you could create in between.

The tightness in her chest began to ease as she sat there. The muscles in her body soon relaxed and after a moment she found her head rolling sideways so that her cheek rested on her upraised knees.

She looked out over the vista of trunks before her. From her vantage point on the ground, she could see very little without straining her neck. Not worth it. A breeze she hadn't realized was there rippled through the leaves and touched her clammy skin.

She heard him then, the light, quick steps as he ran toward her.

She should have moved so he wouldn't see her. Instead, she just sat there and waited.

HE REACHED DOWN, WRAPPED both hands around her upper arms and pulled her off the ground. And straight into his arms.

"Don't run away from me again."

"I didn't—"

Her protest was cut off by the press of his mouth to hers. The kiss consumed her, turning her knees to water and knocking everything else away.

Everything except the feel of him.

However, when he let her up for a brief snatch of air

the words were right where she'd left them, on the tip of her tongue.

"I was never the one to run away, Luke. That was always you."

With a growl of protest—whether at her words or at the truth of them she wasn't certain—he crushed his mouth to hers again. One thing was for sure. He had better plans for her mouth than speech.

His tongue thrust deep inside, sparring with her. His lips were hard, savage at first. She wasn't sure what or who he was fighting. Certainly not her. Did she want to blast him for turning away from her? Absolutely. But she couldn't think of what she needed to say.

Did he expect her to protest that this wasn't right? It wasn't. But apparently, that didn't matter much. Not to her body that cried out at even the thought of letting him go.

She scraped her teeth across his bottom lip, fighting back, refusing to just give in and let go. Nipping down hard on his tongue, not enough to draw blood but enough to tell him she was far from the shy and obedient girl she'd once been. He'd find it hard to dominate her, even with his strength and experience giving him the upper hand.

Ainsley wrapped one leg high above his hip, the heel of her foot digging into the small of his back and push-ing his body closer. She grabbed handfuls of hair at the nape of his neck and tugged him tight to her body. She wasn't gentle and knew that when she did let go strands of his dark hair would be intertwined with her fingers.

His hands scraped down both sides of her back, arching her body into his, straining her spine for that last final inch that would bring them closer.

Pulling away, she let her head drop back, her neck needing relief as much as her lungs needed an intake of breath.

This time, there were no words. They needed none. Their hands and eyes and lips spoke for them. They both understood, consumed by something neither of them really wanted. Unable to deny themselves or each other.

The night seemed to close in around them. The breeze stilled. Sound stopped. Even the moon disappeared, leaving them lost in a space devoid of anything but each other.

Luke's hot mouth trailed down the open invitation of her throat. He nipped and licked and breathed her in. She raised her head to watch him, enjoying the glitter of desire deep in his eyes as he watched back.

He was still naked and she could feel his erection pressed tight to the center of her sex. The thin running shorts she'd pulled on were little protection against the heat and insistency of him.

He was hard and tight against her and the nylon was quickly slippery with the evidence of her own desire. The scrape and friction as it worked against her was becoming unbearable.

Even as her focus settled squarely where she wanted him most, Luke seemed perfectly happy to draw out the experience. Somewhere in the moments of her distraction, he'd gone from harsh and hungry to soft and persuasive.

His mouth, no longer savage, was coaxing and gentle as he eased it from the center of her throat to the edge of her collarbone, stopped only by the worn neck of her threadbare T-shirt.

His fingers curled in the neck, stretching it away from her body to give him better access to her skin.

His lips followed, feather-light kisses that did nothing but make her burn hotter. They were just above her aching breasts beneath the waiting cloth. Where she wanted him most, he couldn't reach.

As he strained toward her, his tongue licking out across her skin like a snake's seeking warmth, she let out a whimper of frustration.

His chuckle snapped her head up so she could look into his eyes and see the mischief there. The sharp edge of his half smile told her everything she needed to know.

He was doing it on purpose.

Hell-bent on thwarting him, Ainsley reached down for the hem of her T-shirt, ready to take it off and remove his avenue of torture. Before she could, he shook his head, crumpled the neck tight in both fists and ripped.

The material tore beneath his hands as easily as a piece of paper and fluttered to her feet.

She stood there, speechless for about three seconds before saying, "I liked that shirt, damn you."

"Not as much as you'll like this."

His words brushed across her skin a second before his teeth clamped tight around her waiting nipple. Her body arched, a combination of blinding pleasure and pain that made her want to scream. But she wouldn't give him the satisfaction. That was precisely what he hoped for.

Even as she bit back the response, her nails dug into the tender flesh of his neck, her body arching into his mouth, as she urged him closer.

But two could definitely play at this game.

Reaching down she wrapped her hand around the length of his erection and squeezed. His breath backed up into his lungs; she could see the swell of his ribs, could feel the snap of tension as it whipped through his body. "Heathen," he whispered against her, but she could also feel the stretch of his smile against her skin. "When did you become such a hellcat?"

"There are a lot of things you don't know about me."

The most important of which was that she was quickly approaching the end of her rope. It had been a long time since she'd had sex and she was walking a tightrope of not wanting it to end and needing the release so badly she thought she'd die without it.

As if he could sense the urgency pulling on her, he reached down, wrapped both of her legs around his waist and backed her up until she was flush against the trunk of the tree that just minutes ago had been her sanctuary. Now it was the springboard for the most pleasure she'd experienced in longer than she cared to remember.

The rough bark bit into her skin. In the morning she'd be covered in scratches. Right now, she didn't give a damn.

What she did care about was the way he pressed into her body, the hard length of his erection sitting just where she needed it most. Her sex burned, an ache that only he could ease. And he was so close. Relief was so close. All that stood in the way of that moment were the flimsy shorts she still wore.

"Condom?"

And the realization that neither of them had birth control. It wasn't as if she'd expected this to happen when she'd thrown on her running clothes. And even if Luke had...his clothes were still at the pond apparently.

With a groan, she shook her head. "Sonofabitch."

Luke let out a shocked laugh, more a burst of sound and air than amusement. "My thoughts exactly."

As he eased away from her, she thought he was going to let her go...end it all right here, right now. Her body protested, her hands clinging to his arms, a whimper leaking through her parted lips.

What surprised her was his moving back in, whispering, "Shh," against her lips. He wasn't going to leave her panting and burning.

His hand made its way beneath the thin barrier of cloth, finding the slippery heart of her sex. Her world almost imploded simply from his touch. Her vision grayed at the edges and her eyes automatically slid shut. She wasn't sure if she still breathed...wasn't sure it mattered one way or the other. If she died now, like this, then at least she would be happy.

A single finger slipped inside her, and then another.

The walls of her sex spasmed on the pleasure of the intrusion.

He began to work her, slowly at first, but quickly realizing that she was so close to the edge it wouldn't take much. His fingers slid in and out, his thumb rubbed the nub of flesh above. Her body tightened, fighting for and against what he offered her.

Her hips pumped against him, her back pushing tight into the trunk of the tree. Pain and pleasure mingled so tightly she couldn't tell where one began and the other ended.

He whispered in her ear, words she couldn't decipher, words that didn't matter. She only knew he pushed her on, higher, harder, faster.

A scream erupted from her throat as her body quaked and gave in to what he wanted, gave in to him.

The release was staggering. The best orgasm she'd ever had. But it wasn't enough. Even as her mind floated away she knew there was more.

She was unsatisfied. She wanted Luke. And she wanted him now.

NEED POUNDED THROUGH his body, like the ebb and flow of a tide, sucking against the sand and pulling it out to sea. His desire for her was a living thing, a force he couldn't possibly conquer.

And he needed her now.

More than this childish grope in the dark, he wanted to see her, feel her, taste and consume her.

He wanted everything she'd give him.

And then he wanted more.

She still sagged against the tree, her eyes closed, her lungs sucking in air. He could wait for her to recover, coax her into coming back to his room where he had a handful of condoms.

But why?

She might come to her senses and decide that they'd gone far enough, or think what they'd done so far was a mistake. He wasn't taking that chance.

Leaning down, he swept her legs out from under her, toppling her back into his other arm, and crushed her to his body.

Her squeak of surprise might have been funny, if he'd been coherent enough to notice. What he did perceive was the way she wrapped her arms around him, clinging to him and pulling herself even closer into his hold.

She shifted against him, rolling her body so that her breasts pressed solidly against his bare chest and her face buried snugly into the crook of his neck. He could feel the rise and fall of her breaths against his skin, the tormenting rub as her nipples slid up and down his chest.

Her breath touched him, moist and light, a tickle of sensation that drove him absolutely mad. She could reach out with her mouth, her fingers, anything. But she didn't. She simply let the moist air through her tempting lips caress him.

He strode across the orchard. They weren't far from the house; he could see the faint lights from the upstairs windows, his room and hers. Four minutes, tops, and they'd be there together, taking up where they'd left off.

"I can walk, you know."

It was almost the first thing she'd said to him from the moment she'd laid eyes on his naked body.

"I'm not taking that chance. I let you down, you might run away."

Her body tensed in his arms but he had no idea why. Was she frightened? Angry? Disappointed?

"And that would be bad?"

There, in the single tremor on the last word, the only giveaway of the vulnerability she was excellent at hiding. He hated to see that vulnerability, a reminder of the terrible childhood he couldn't change for her. There was one sure way to make it disappear…if only for a little while.

Shifting his hold on her thighs, he slid a single finger beneath the edge of her nylon running shorts and thrilled at her muffled intake of breath.

"Very bad."

He pushed into the house, the old front door banging against the wall with a protesting creak at their abrupt entry.

"Shh," she hissed into his ear. "You'll wake Gran."

Oh, wouldn't that have been a sight. He was naked as the day he was born, his skin still damp and sticky from the water that hadn't quite dried yet. Ainsley's feet were streaked with mud, her breasts swinging free. And he was clomping them both through the house like a herd of buffalo.

"She sleeps like the dead." He would know. He'd used that fact to his advantage many times in his misspent youth.

"Not funny, Luke."

No, probably not. He strode up the stairs with her, skipping the noisy fourth stair just to avoid another protest from her and made it to the hallway without so much as a sound coming from his grandmother's room at the head of the stairs.

He didn't stop to ask; he simply strode into his own room and laid her gently across the bed.

The covers were rumpled beneath her where he'd tossed and turned in the night. Pale white cotton sheets only emphasized the luster of her skin. She rarely wore makeup. She didn't have to. Her skin seemed to glow from within, creamy and bronzed by the sun.

She stretched out before him, and he was almost overwhelmed with the realization that he was about to touch her again. For the past eight years, memories, dreams and sometimes nightmares had haunted him—the need for her had been so strong. Over those years no other woman had ever come close to what he'd had—what he wanted again—with Ainsley. He'd second-guessed his decisions, wondered whether the sacrifice he'd made was worth what he'd gained.

In his heart he'd always thought the answer was no. But it hadn't done him any good to acknowledge his mistake, not when she couldn't be his anyway.

But now, tonight, she was his. Completely and totally.

No past. No twin brother to come between them. Nothing but the here and now.

A flash of uncertainty crossed her face, making him realize he'd been staring too long.

But she was so beautiful. He just couldn't seem to find the words to tell her.

She jolted sideways, fumbling in the covers to try and find a shield against him. He couldn't have that. Sinking down beside her, he reached for the knotted sheet and pulled it out of her grasp before she could do anything with it.

He leaned in; she retreated back, propped high on her elbows in the center of his bed. He followed.

The chill of her skin registered. It should have been a balm to the sizzling heat, but it just made the burn worse.

He reached for her, running the backs of his fingers down her side, over the curve of her breast and down her ribs.

She shivered and goose bumps flowed across her skin. He moved closer, following the trail with the edge of his lips, not quite touching, barely breathing. "Beautiful."

A strangled sound buzzed in the back of her throat, a cross between a protest and the expression of her own need.

"Yes. You're beautiful. You always have been and you always will be. Gorgeous. Simple. Perfect."

She looked into his eyes, her face so close to his own now that all he could see were the round, blue pools.

And the belief that they held. The belief that he spoke the truth.

He watched them melt, darken, deepen and begin to glitter. The corners tipped up, changing the expression on her face from wide-eyed wonder to one of understanding, power and expectation.

She wanted this. She wanted him. And he was going to delight in fulfilling her every desire....

9

How could she still be on fire? How could she still want this man? Not just after already having been sated but after all that they'd been through, everything he'd done…and not done.

But she did want him. And Ainsley knew to the depths of her soul that the emotions bubbling up inside her weren't going to go away. As long as he was here, next to her, walking the same ground and sleeping under the same roof, the buzz in her blood would only get stronger.

He reached for her and she let him.

It would be easy, in the bright light of day, to convince herself that he'd seduced her. That he'd played on old fantasies and the embers of the desire they once shared.

But she wouldn't.

At this moment, she was precisely where she wanted to be. In Luke's arms.

And the chances of that ever happening again were

slim to none. If life had taught her anything, it was to seize the moment.

But what she really wanted to seize was him.

There was nothing wrong with knowing that and weighing it against the potential for pain later. She'd made a decision and there was no going back. There would be no regrets.

Part of her, the innately honest and nurturing part, almost spoke to make sure that Luke understood what this encounter was, a fleeting chance at pleasure for them both.

And then she remembered who was about to share her bed. Luke had no designs on anything with her beyond this night.

Somehow the realization that there was no future relationship to worry about set her free. She could be as uninhibited and daring as she wanted.

And suddenly, she wanted to be very daring.

Laying her palm flat against his naked chest, Ainsley pushed back against Luke, holding him at arm's length. The molten heat in his eyes quickly cooled to concern and confusion. The tiny imp inside her—the one she rarely let out—gleefully enjoyed Luke's discomfort.

She'd set him off balance and that was a rare occurrence with Luke Collier.

Applying pressure to his shoulders and invading his space, she urged him down to the bed as she rose up and over him. His body folded beneath her, like a collapsible box. They moved together in harmony as if the change in position had been choreographed.

She straddled his body as he looked up at her; for once he was the vulnerable one. She could do anything she wanted. Or so she told herself. She could walk away. She could torture him until they both whimpered. She could indulge in every fantasy she'd ever had in those dark and lonely nights without him.

But she wouldn't do any of those things. Not now. Now she simply wanted to indulge—herself and him. She longed to feel him, explore his body as he'd explored hers in the orchard. She wanted to know him again as intimately as she had before.

Running her hands down the length of his torso, she relished the way he arched into her touch. The way his eyes glittered as he silently watched her luxuriate in his masculinity.

The sprinkling of hair across his chest tickled the palms of her hands. The sensation was its own caress— one she never would have counted as sensual, yet somehow it was.

She leaned down to rain tiny kisses across his skin. The ticklish sides of his ribs, the sensitive discs of his puckered nipples, the flat plane of his belly. Every place she touched he instantly responded to her with jumping muscles, guttural groans and the eager jerk of his insistent erection.

She dropped her mouth lower, running just the tip of her tongue down the length of his sex. It wasn't enough— for him or for her. But judging by his sharp intake of breath and the heat of her own spreading arousal, they both enjoyed the torment.

She scooted back on her knees to give herself unfettered access to what she wanted to play with most. She let the side of her tongue rub slowly up the length of his cock again, looking into his eyes just as she reached the sensitive head. His fingers fisted the sheets beside his body, rumpling them into a tight ball and popping the elastic away from the bed.

That small sound seemed to galvanize her. It was proof of the short leash he had on his control. She wanted to feel and hear that leash snap just for her.

Bending down, she took him into her mouth. Sucking him deep, she worked hard on his sex as she let him slip back out. She used her fingers and tongue, lips and teeth to tantalize and destroy them both.

When he finally reached for her, his fingers digging just as roughly into her skin as they had into the bed, he had her flat on her back and beneath him in seconds. The room whirled around her with the speed of her transition.

He crushed his body to hers, bringing them skin-to-skin and wrenching a moan from her throat. She realized this was the first time she'd fully touched him. Up until this point they'd been playing, tormenting each other. Now he was wholly against her and she wanted more. All of him.

"Condom." She panted the word on a labored breath.

"Drawer." His level of speech seemed to match hers. Somewhere in the back of her mind she found that gratifying. To know that she could affect him just as much as he affected her. That they could do this to each other.

His hand worked between them, forcing air where there hadn't been any. He found her sex, wet, swollen and ready for him. He slipped a single finger inside and she arched against him, her muscles pulsing around his invasion.

Ainsley blindly reached to the bedside table, opening the drawer and pulling out a condom from the package stashed there.

Her movements were jerky, her brain half-possessed with the pleasure he was drawing from her. But she wanted him so she was on a mission.

Ripping into the package, she reached for him, letting her fingers slide along the length of him as she rolled the condom down.

He was right there, at her entrance, ready to put her out of her misery. She was open to him, legs splayed, muscles straining, hips gyrating. And yet they both waited, prolonging the moment and drawing out the pleasure. As if they both feared this was their only chance.

Finally, she'd had enough. Flinging his hand away from her, she guided him to her center and waited for him to slide home.

He didn't disappoint. But then, he never had. He thrust inside her. It took her a moment to stretch and accommodate him but once she did...

Her mind blurred, her body focusing on the single point where they connected. It was perfect; they were perfect together. He slid out again, drawing a whimper from her when she lost the sensation of him deep inside. She wanted him back again. She wanted him with her.

Ainsley wrapped her legs high around his hips, pushing her heels into his body and driving him back to her. Her hips thrust upward and the internal muscles of her sex clenched him, pulling even more pleasure from the friction of their play.

He whispered nonsense words into the cloud of her hair but the urgency and desperation in them were clear to her. Their echo deep inside her.

His hands brushed from her sides, down her arms, seeking something he couldn't seem to find. Until his searching fingers twined with her own, bringing her hands up over her head.

The strength of his hold and the position of her body forced her tighter against him, bringing them closer together than she'd ever thought possible. His mouth found hers in the rush of pleasure and abandon, another connection between them.

His hold on her hands tightened, an unvoiced urging she wanted so much to obey and ignore all at once. The muscles of her sex began to quiver with the beginning throb of her release anyway. She tried to hold it off, tried to steal one more moment. But as his tongue and cock thrust deep into her body in unison, she lost all control.

The pleasure of him inside her again was just too much.

She bucked against him, pulsing and pulling as her body exploded, milking every last second of bliss she could get. If this was it, she wanted it all, whatever he'd give her. Whatever she could take.

Aftershocks were still racking her when a guttural

groan of satisfaction burst from Luke's lips. He ground into the open cradle of her thighs as his hips pumped into her with masculine abandon.

Her eyes threatened to flutter shut as the force of his release had her spasming on an echo of what he'd already given her.

Neither of them said anything as he rolled off, tucking her tight into the curve of his body and bringing the covers up over them both. There were no words, nothing left to say. Not in this moment.

Right now it was enough that his arms were tight across her stomach, holding her close to his warmth. Right now it was enough that they were together.

She was too exhausted to do anything anyway. Tomorrow would be soon enough to face the consequences of their actions.

SHE WOKE UP. ALONE. In Luke's bed.

The sensation was…unsettling. If he'd been beside her it might have been worse.

At least this way she could deal with the aftermath of her rash decisions alone.

Did she regret it? Not yet, but maybe eventually. For now, her body was too sated for regrets.

Stretching her arms over her head, Ainsley arched her back and relished the twinge of her stiff and sore muscles. She couldn't resist a contented smile.

She hadn't felt this good in…ever.

"Well, if that isn't a cat-eating-the-canary grin I don't know what is." His words were a lazy drawl that startled the hell out of her. She jackknifed in the bed, reflexively grabbing for the covers to make sure she was decent.

The warmth of his chuckle oozed down her spine. "I think it's a little late for modesty."

He was braced in the doorway, arms crossed over his chest, one wide shoulder holding him up. A worn pair of denims rode low on his hips, threatening to slip off.

Her mouth went dry and her tongue swelled to about five times its normal size. At least it felt that way. She hadn't been tongue-tied and helpless since she was eight. But the sight of him, rumpled and sexy, about did her in.

Her heart raced, a combination of nerves and a desire to revisit what they'd shared last night. She had no idea what to say to him. The heat of a blush began to creep up her skin; she could feel the sting of it and wanted to smack herself.

Pushing away from the door frame, Luke walked toward her. "It's late. Gran's been up for a while but I thought you might need the sleep." A smile touched the edges of his lips briefly. It fascinated her, that smile that wasn't quite there. It was something she'd never seen him do before. In the past he'd been larger than life. He'd never censored anything, his thoughts, his emotions, his desires, his laughter. Everything with him had always been on the surface for everyone to see.

She was beginning to realize that wasn't the case anymore.

"We need to leave for the service in an hour or so."

His words brought a cloud over her thoughts. She'd

been so wrapped up in the experience of last night that she'd forgotten what today brought with it—for him and for her.

His eyes dulled for a second before he reached for her and kissed her. She had almost no warning that it was coming. The kiss held the quiet power of connection, the leashed control of unfulfilled desire and the promise of more…later.

Luke let her go. Pulling back, he stood up from the bed and stared down at her, blinked and then was gone.

She sat there, slightly shaken and unsure of exactly what had just happened as she listened to his footsteps retreat down the worn stairs. She was so confused. By herself—her own desires and hopes and complicated dreams. By him—what he thought this was, what he thought he wanted.

Shaking her head, Ainsley realized now was not the time to contemplate all of this. In a little while she'd be playing hostess to half the county as everyone paid their last respects to Pops.

Right now, that's what she needed to worry about. She could figure out the rest later.

Leaping from the bed, she saw a neat pile of her clothes sitting on the chair in the corner. Shorts, a T-shirt, bra and panties. Definitely not what she'd been wearing last night.

Another blush suffused her skin at the thought of Luke rummaging through her drawers. She didn't ever really think about her wardrobe. Not much reason to when she spent so much time outdoors getting dirty, sticky and sweaty. But for once she was embarrassed. What had he seen? What had he thought?

However, that embarrassment was quickly overshadowed by another.

What had happened to her clothes from last night? His?

She could just imagine one of the seasonal workers coming across her ripped T-shirt beneath the peach trees. Or worse finding Luke's shorts and shirt in a pile by the pond.

What would they think?

It took Ainsley less than a minute to decide it didn't matter. She wasn't ashamed of anything she'd done last night.

Given the chance, she'd do it all again.

It remained to be seen whether she'd get that chance.

THE CEREMONY WAS A BLUR. A whirlwind of people, stories, memories and tears. The oppressive heat and the advanced age of most of Pops's friends meant the contingency that followed the hearse up the seldom-used gravel path to the family grave site was smaller. Most people had elected to stay inside the air-conditioned chapel at the church.

Ainsley sat beside Luke in the limo the funeral home had provided for the family. Gran sat on the opposite seat, across from them both. She looked tired and forlorn and he wished there was something he could do to help. But there wasn't. Nothing he could say or do would bring back the man she'd loved for most of her life. She might have had a chance to prepare for the separation but it was clear that she felt his loss down to her soul. He'd never seen her so pale and…motionless. In all his memories she'd been a firecracker of a woman, able to bend every one of the men in her life to her will, either with honey or with vinegar—whichever the situation required.

He hated seeing her this way. It made him feel powerless.

Ainsley wasn't much better. He didn't think she'd moved from the moment she'd sat down beside him. Not a twitch, a cough, a fidget. She'd just turned her head and stared out the window as they'd driven the few miles onto the family property.

He knew she had loved Pops; he was the only grandfather-figure she'd ever known. And Pops had always thought of her as part of the family.

Luke wondered if her melancholy was entirely due to his grandfather's passing. He wondered if this drive brought back memories of Logan's death.

And he hated himself for the brief spurt of jealousy that flared at the thought. But before he'd even come to terms with it, his jealousy was overridden by a sense of loss so deep he almost doubled over in pain. Thinking of his twin, when he was about to bury another person he'd loved deeply was just too much. He closed his eyes, took a breath and tried to pushed Logan's memory away. He couldn't deal with both of them right now.

The funeral home had set up a tent and a single row of chairs before the prepared coffin suspended over the waiting hole in the ground. The tent kept the sun from beating down directly on their heads, but it did nothing about the suffocating humidity in the air. Before they'd even taken their seats, Luke could feel his white dress shirt sticking to his sweat-soaked back beneath his suit jacket.

At least Ainsley had decided to wear a basic black dress with filmy sleeves that barely covered the curve of her shoulder. He probably should have been paying attention to the preacher's words. Instead, his eyes fell to her toes peeking out of strappy sandals. They were painted a suitably conservative shade of pale pink. For one unnerving moment he had the urge to reach down and run his lips across the row.

Completely inappropriate but much easier to deal with than the reality before him.

He'd never been good at goodbyes. It never got easier.

He and Pops might not have always seen eye-to-eye but he'd loved his grandfather. Until this moment he hadn't realized just how much the loss would hurt.

Jerking his gaze back to the preacher, a nice Southern man with a sizable paunch and a face turned red and glistening from the heat. The man gestured for Gran to move forward, leading the line of people who would leave a single white rose on top of the coffin.

They filed out, the sun hitting Luke squarely in the face, leaving him blind and disoriented for several seconds. It was Ainsley's soft murmur and the touch of her hand on his arm that called him back.

"Gran asked that we stay and see everyone gone. She needed to head into the house. Heat. Grief."

Her eyes bright blue and moist with the tears she refused to shed, she looked up at him, waiting for his agreement.

At that moment, what he wanted most in the world was to crush her to his chest, hold her tight and let her ease the sharp ache that had settled in the center of his chest.

But he wouldn't.

Instead, he nodded. She let go of his arm and stood beside him as the few neighbors and friends who had come drifted away to their waiting cars.

He heard the creak of the crank behind him as the staff from the funeral home lowered his grandfather's coffin into the ground, and had to leave. He couldn't watch.

He began walking, with no destination, just the single-minded thought of getting away.

Before he realized it, he was across the graveyard, in the section that held his parents' and brother's graves.

He paused first beside his mother's headstone and then his father's. After so many years, he could barely even remember what their voices had sounded like or the shape of their eyes or the feel of their hands running over his hair. They had been with him for such a short time, that their memory had begun to fade long ago. He missed them, in an abstract sort of way. He missed what a mother and father would have given him—security, love, connection. But he'd received those things from other people in his life. He was certain their loss would have been harder if he'd been older when they'd died.

But Logan. Logan's memory would always be sharp in his mind. Logan, the brother he'd shared everything with. Logan, the other half to his existence.

This time, instead of moonlight, bright sunlight shone down over the stone as he ran his hand across the curved edge of the white granite.

The sunlight glared off the surface. It should have been happy and playful—just as Logan had been—but it wasn't.

"He missed you. Terribly."

He hadn't realized Ainsley had followed him, but he should have known she would. Even if this place held sad memories for her, she'd never leave him to deal with his alone…unless he asked her to.

He wouldn't. Just knowing she was there somehow eased the burden of the day. More than it should. But he wouldn't look a gift horse in the mouth. At least not right now.

Her hand joined his on the stone, not touching, just resting beside him, proof that if nothing else, they shared this.

"Every other word out of his mouth was *Luke*." She laughed a low, strangled sound as if it hurt just to let it out. "He was so proud of you."

For the second time that day, Luke found himself choking back emotion. He walked away from Logan's grave, unable even to look at the cold stone, all that was left of his twin.

He didn't make it far, only to the next grave over. He stared down, unseeing for several seconds, his eyes blurred with emotions he wouldn't release.

Gradually, he got himself under control and became aware of exactly what he was looking at.

Ainsley had gone strangely still beside him, her hand half-outstretched as if to bring him back to her side. His eyes jumped to hers, to the stricken look that filled them, before slamming back to the marker in front of him.

It was smaller than Logan's but made of the same white granite. There was an angel, a cherub, carved into the center, the depiction of a chubby-cheeked, bright-eyed and laughing child with wings and a harp. Beneath the cherub were the words:

For my angel,
May you now fly.

Beneath that were three words and a single date, Alexander Lucas Collier, August 30, 2002.

The same day that Logan had died.

10

OH, GOD. SHE KNEW THIS wasn't good. She could tell by the expression on his face that Luke had begun to draw his own conclusions.

She'd known, in her heart she'd known, that she was going to have to tell him. But she wasn't ready, not today.

"Whose headstone is this?"

He stalked toward her, his eyes changing from bleak to angry.

He reached for her, grabbing her by the arms and pulling her up onto the tips of her toes. She thought he might shake her. She could see the roiling emotions clouding his eyes, watched as his teeth gritted against the words when he asked her again. "Whose headstone is that?"

But he didn't shake her. His grip on her arms, though tight enough she couldn't break it, didn't actually hurt. She almost wished that it did.

She wanted to drop her eyes; she wanted to disconnect from him as she told him the truth, but she couldn't.

Something in his expression wouldn't let her take the coward's way out.

"My son's."

"Your…" His voice trailed off. He eased his grip enough that her heels touched down. She knew he hadn't realized he was pulling her up to him. His head whipped around, his eyes flashed as he reread the few meager lines on the stone.

And then he looked at her again.

Now, tempering the anger was an edge of concern… concern for her. Part of her would have liked to accept that compassion but she knew she couldn't. Not until he knew the full truth. Until then it wasn't real.

"What happened?"

She took a deep breath, her mind racing. "You know I was injured in the accident. I went into premature labor. They couldn't save me and the baby, and Alex was too young to survive." This time she did lower her gaze to his chest, too overwhelmed with the emotions she'd experienced in those days and weeks immediately following the accident. "So young. A few more weeks and they might have saved him." The agony of that had haunted her for years. She'd never quite been able to forgive herself for her inability to protect her child, even when he was supposed to be safe inside her body.

His grip on her tightened again.

"How young?"

She was bewildered by his question for a moment. It wasn't what she'd expected and she'd been lost in a past she could never change.

And then she realized exactly what he was asking her.

She opened her mouth to tell him that he had been Alex's father. But the words refused to leave her mouth. Instead she answered his question. "Twenty-four weeks."

"Twenty-four…" He trailed off and again she tried to tell him but the words seemed stuck somewhere between her throat and her heart.

"Lucas. Did Logan ask you to name him after me?"

Shaking her head she said, "No." She finally met his eyes again.

They were a storm, so conflicted. She could feel her throat tighten, knowing that this was about to change everything.

Just when she'd finally gotten him back.

Although, she hadn't really, had she? He had no intention of staying here. Of making her a part of his life. No more than he'd had those eight years ago. She'd run out of time. The piper was here and he demanded his price. The problem was, that price was going to be higher than she'd expected. But then, that's usually how the story ended.

"I chose the name because Alex was yours."

His.

The word registered in his brain but it didn't sink in right away.

His son.

Luke whirled around and stared at the small white stone again. It was the same, and yet, now it looked completely different.

His son.

How had this happened? How had he not known? Hell, how had he not even known she was pregnant?

He hadn't realized he'd voiced the questions aloud until Ainsley answered them. Or maybe he hadn't said anything and she was simply filling in the voids.

"I didn't know until after you'd left." Her words penetrated the fog that seemed to wrap his body and brain. It was insulating. Somehow comforting. He knew that it was protecting him from the emotions he should be feeling…anger, betrayal, grief. More grief. Just what he needed today.

As if in slow motion, he turned back to her, wanted to see her face as she explained how he'd had a son he'd never even known existed. Had existed.

The pain started then, knifing through the fog. He'd gained and lost a child in the space of a few minutes. How could it hurt so much?

Ainsley reached for him, almost touching his arm before he shifted away. With a pinched expression, she dropped her hand.

"I had no idea where you were. How to contact you. For weeks. Months."

"So you turned to my brother? For what? Help? Solace? A warm body at night?"

Her eyes flickered for a moment, anger glistening in their depths before the emotion disappeared, replaced by pain. He didn't want to see her pain. He didn't want to think about this from her perspective. Not now.

"For help. My father threw me out. It was a tough

pregnancy. I was ordered to get bed rest if I didn't want
to risk losing the baby. I had nowhere to turn. I came to
the orchard one day hoping Logan could tell me where
you were...."

"And stayed. We were twins, after all. One of us was
just as good as the other, I suppose." He heard the wasp-
ish tone of his own voice, the sting behind his words.
Even as he said them he realized they weren't true, but
he didn't take them back.

Ainsley flinched, before quickly regaining her composure. She stood before him, shoulders squared, spine
straight, head held high.

"You know it wasn't like that. He offered me a place
to stay, a family, safety and medical care for me and
Alex. I was desperate and in no position to refuse. I had
a child to think of. It wasn't what I wanted. It was what
the baby and I both needed."

The calm way she relayed the reasons behind her
decision—noble and maternal reasons—made his jaw
ache with tension.

He could see her, alone, scared, afraid of losing her
child, making the logical decision for them both. So
Ainsley. Practical down to her pale pink toes.

At the moment he hated that practicality though part
of him could understand and appreciated her protective
instincts toward their son.

He certainly hadn't been available to help. But he
would have been. If he'd known.

"Why didn't you tell me? When I called home? When
I came for the funeral?"

She closed her eyes and raised her head to the heavens. The corners of her eyes wrinkled as she squeezed them tight, as if in pain, as if in thought. When she finally answered, she continued to stare up into the bright sky instead of looking at him.

"We fought. Logan and I, that day. About telling you. He wanted me to call you. But…I wasn't ready. I was still angry. I knew I needed to work through that before I called. That once I told you, you'd be part of my life forever. I was going to… I just wanted a little more time. I had months before the baby was born. I thought."

Her voice clogged, growing thick with emotion. He wasn't sure if she was trying to hold back tears. It would make no difference. They wouldn't sway him. Not now.

"Then it didn't matter. Logan was dead. Alex was gone. I was in so much pain and so heartsick. And you didn't come." She finally dropped her eyes, but instead of looking him in the face, she studied the ground at his feet.

"It seemed cruel at that point to tell you. It couldn't change anything. It would only cause you the same grief I was fighting. You had a life. Away from me. Away from here."

He wanted to grab her and shake her. He wanted to pull her into his arms and soothe the pain he could see stamped across every feature of her face. She'd lost so much. And borne the brunt of immeasurable pain…on her own. When it should have been theirs to share.

He was angry. Angry she hadn't told him, then and now. But she'd been dealing with so much. All alone.

Fragile, competent, practical Ainsley.

He opened his mouth to absolve her, but his jaw snapped shut instead. He couldn't do that. Not yet. He would. He wanted to. But not yet.

He had one more question to ask first.

He stepped forward, grasping her by the arms again and forcing her to stop avoiding his eyes. "Why didn't you tell me during the time we just spent together?"

She finally looked at him.

Her eyes swam with unshed tears that seemed to magnify the swirling emotions roiling inside her. The despair, the guilt, the fear, the anger, the betrayal…the hope. He could read them all as they seemed to slam into the center of his chest, a tight ball of fury that almost made him take a step back.

And then she answered.

"Because I…I didn't know how." Her words were barely a whisper. He leaned closer. "I didn't want to hurt you. I didn't want to take someone else from your life."

AINSLEY STARED AT THE ceiling, her head lay against the curved back of the rocking chair in the corner of the living room. It was dark. Gran had gone to bed an hour or two ago, after they'd shared a quiet, simple dinner. Alone.

Neither of them had said much. They'd both been preoccupied with the events of the day.

Ainsley hadn't seen Luke since he'd walked away from

her, leaving her standing between Logan's and Alexander's graves. Feeling deeper despair than she'd experienced in a very long time.

He'd been back in her life for less than a week and despite everything she'd known—the past, his inflexibility, the life he had waiting for him and the secret that was a gaping chasm between them—she'd let him back in. Into her heart, into her life and into her body.

Stupid, stupid, stupid.

He probably hated her now. And she couldn't completely blame him. In his situation, she'd probably hate her, too. Sure, she had reasons…but in the dark they seemed inconsequential.

As day had faded to night, she hadn't bothered to turn on any lights. There was little moonlight outside to dispel the gloom that seemed to settle around her. That was how he found her, sitting in the dark, staring up at the ceiling, her feet pushing rhythmically against the floor as she rocked.

Ainsley knew he was there the minute he stepped into the house. Even if the creaking floorboards and the metallic clang of the screen door hadn't alerted her to his arrival, she seemed to have a sixth sense where he was concerned. The muscles in her body tensed as his footsteps brought him closer. She didn't have to see him to know that Luke was home.

She expected him to pass her by. Aside from the soft snick of the wooden runners against the floor, there was no indication that anyone was even in the room. Besides, she figured she was the last person he'd want to see right now.

She was wrong.

He found her with the unerring accuracy of someone with his own built-in radar.

He watched her for several seconds, standing just inside the doorway to the room. He could turn around and walk away. Or he could come inside. The choice was his. She'd said everything she could possibly say this afternoon. It was his turn now.

Whatever happened, he deserved the right to his response. She wouldn't take that away from him. She'd already taken more than she'd had any right to.

"I need to send the financial paperwork to the broker tomorrow. I know you've been preoccupied for the past couple days but do you have it done?"

She squeezed her eyes shut for a moment, then opened them again. The ceiling hadn't changed colors. There weren't suddenly spots or stripes or plaid there. And yet, she still felt as if her world had shifted somehow with his simple question.

If he wanted to pretend nothing had happened, then she supposed she'd honor his wishes.

"I'll have it for you in the morning."

Her voice sounded rusty and uneven to her own ears. She hoped he couldn't hear the emotions the jagged words covered.

The silence stretched. After several uncomfortable seconds, he took a single step farther into the room. A single step closer to her.

Her body tensed and her feet touched down to the floor and refused to push back off again. The rocker swayed against the loss of steady motion. She didn't look at him, wasn't sure that she wanted to.

"Ainsley."

The word spilled into the space between them.

"Yes?"

"I'm sorry."

11

"YOU HAVE NOTHING TO BE sorry for."

"I do. I left you alone when you needed me most. Not once but twice."

He turned away from her, so she couldn't see directly into his eyes. What she could see was the profile of his face—sharp angles and planes shadowed by the night that seemed to blanket them, to cocoon them together rather than keep them apart.

"You know the worst part? Logan was here for you. He did what I should have done. I should be grateful. Instead, I'm so angry and jealous. He got to experience those moments with you, hearing the baby's heartbeat, feeling him kick for the first time. He's dead and I'm still jealous."

They were the most stark and honest words she thought she'd ever heard him say. Luke had always been boisterous and charming. What he hadn't been was open and free with his emotions…even with her. Even with Logan.

He'd always held a piece of himself back, protected, safe.

She'd understood what motivated that need and had hoped that in time he'd learn to trust her. Learn that she wasn't going to disappear the way his parents had.

But, instead, he'd turned his back on everything they'd had together. Perhaps if she'd pushed…

No, it didn't help to rehash a past she couldn't change. At this moment, she was grateful for the small glimpse of himself that he'd finally shown her.

She stood up and reached for him, laying her hand along the curve of his arm simply to show him that she was here, beside him.

"You can yell at me if it helps. You can get it out and work through it. Logan is gone. You can't shout at him. You don't have that chance for catharsis. But you have to know that everything he did was for you, Luke. He did it because he knew you would have if you were here. He was your stand-in."

"As always." He turned his head and looked down at her. His eyes were dark, shaded by both the swirling emotions and the gloom around them. "Don't fool yourself. He did it for you. Logan always loved you. I just didn't realize how much."

She couldn't argue with him about that. Where Luke had kept pieces of himself hidden, Logan had been as transparent as glass with her.

And yet, she still hadn't been able to love him back. He'd been the opposite of everything Luke was, everything she should have wanted after he'd broken her heart.

But in the end, Luke was what she'd wanted. Luke was *still* what she needed.

She recognized that instinct, deep inside him, that told him to protect himself. She'd felt the same way all her life. She'd tried to build a hard core that was inviolate, safe from her father's harsh criticisms and demands. A place where she hid her deepest wishes and fears, because if her father ever found them, he'd exploit them to inflict the most pain.

To her father, Jesus had suffered, and therefore, she should, too. Strength was forged in pain, in sacrifice, in ruthless demands on the body and mind.

She'd found her strength in spite of his abuse.

Just as Luke had found his in action and a business world she didn't understand and couldn't be a part of.

There was a piece of her that wanted to protect him, to soothe the man she loved.

And there was the center of her own problem.

She loved Luke and she always had. Despite everything that had happened, she always would.

And she'd give him everything she could, anything he needed from her. No matter her personal cost.

She wasn't entirely certain if that made her a fool or a martyr. Either way, it wouldn't change her actions.

She reached for him again, laying her palm against the harsh planes of his face. The rough rasp of stubble against her hand sent a shiver down her spine. Such a simple connection of her skin to his and still she responded. Immediately. It was as if he was a catalyst. She was perfectly controlled Ainsley until he entered her life, then energy and heat poured into her body.

He stared down at her, darkness hiding the feelings behind his eyes. Maybe he didn't want this from her now. But she'd offer it to him anyway. He needed the connection to another human being even if he didn't realize it. She could show him how much he meant to her—even if she could never voice the words.

Taking a step closer, Ainsley pressed the length of her body against him. The offer was obvious. But it was his decision to make.

He paused, not declining but not accepting that offer. She fought disappointment when she realized he was going to refuse. She pulled an unsteady breath through parted lips and took a half step away.

In that moment he erupted around her. With a growl, he reached for her. Pulling her up on tiptoe, he took more than she'd even offered. Not that she minded. Not when she could feel the heat and solid weight of muscle against her.

His mouth found hers, hard, punishing, dominating. Tongue thrusting inside, taking what he wanted, dueling with her even as she melted into him.

His hands moving up and down her back were far from gentle. They were demanding. Insistent. While his touch would hardly leave bruises, there was an edge of pain underlying the pleasure. As if he couldn't let either of them enjoy these moments until he'd fully vented the emotions that had haunted him for hours.

And since she was the source of those emotions she'd let him exorcise them however he needed.

And she had no doubt she'd enjoy the experience.

Could penance involve pleasure? Her father certainly would have argued otherwise. But as desire coursed beneath her skin, Ainsley thought that just maybe it could.

Together they could find absolution, forgiveness and the comfort they should have always offered each other. The relief only he could give her.

He tore at her clothes, straining their seams and threatening to ruin them. Slapping his hands away, with trembling fingers, she unbuttoned her own shirt and let it drop to the floor. She was distracted from finishing the job by the sight of Luke's body being revealed as his own clothes hit the hardwood. He paused long enough to fish a condom from the pocket of his jeans.

They said nothing. No words were necessary. The only sound between them was the heated panting of their ragged breaths.

The floor was hard and cool as they tumbled down, a pile of grappling arms, legs, hands and mouths. They could have moved to the sofa on the far side of the room. Or the rag rug three feet away. Or even the rocking chair.

That would have taken more thought and effort than either of them had to spare. Their only focus was each other.

His fingers scraped down the length of her body, sending pleasure tingling along her skin. He stopped long enough to pinch one of her already-swollen and sensitive nipples. Tweaking, playing, tantalizing. A tug of answering pleasure spiked deep inside her body, an ache so intense and immediate she writhed against him in search of the only relief.

Her nails raked down the center of his chest, snagging for a moment on the puckered flesh of his nipple. His body quaked at the touch. He hissed through his teeth, and his eyes glittered down at her with the promise of retribution.

She didn't wait. Leaning forward Ainsley nipped at the cord of muscle running from his neck to his shoulder. It stood out from his tense body, strained by the power of his own desire, making it an easy target. The tangy taste of his skin burst beneath her tongue, its saltiness overlaying the sharp tinge of desire.

With a growl, Luke grasped her tight and rolled their bodies, placing himself beneath her. His head dropped back against the floor, his neck, throat and chest open and exposed to her. Her legs straddled his body, bracketing the thick muscle of his thighs between her own.

The wet folds of her sex opened up around the length of his cock, the irrefutable evidence of her desire slipping and sliding between them.

He tortured her by thrusting up against the most vulnerable part of her. He grasped her hips, holding her where he wanted her. Even as he appeared to offer her the power position in their loving, he refused to actually yield to her. She wasn't even sure if he realized he was doing it. Controlling her in a way that was titillating and frustrating all at the same time.

He wouldn't let her take what she wanted…what she wanted more than her next breath. But he wouldn't give it to her, either. Instead, he rubbed against her body. Even as the hard ridge of his erection nudged and stimulated her clit, the internal walls of her sex spasmed at emptiness.

She wanted him inside her. Now. With a fierce need that scared and tormented her.

Even as he kept her on the edge, taking her closer and then pulling the reward away, she began to fight him. To scrape, pinch, nip and bite.

She growled, a sound she could swear she had never made in her entire life, and sank her teeth into his shoulder. This was no love bite.

She pulled away from him to stare down at the livid crescent she'd created and immediately felt remorse. Something she was tired of feeling around this man.

But she couldn't ignore the urge to reach down and soothe the hurt anyway. Running her tongue over the spot, she licked at him before pressing the softest kiss there.

It was at that precise moment that he reared up and gave her exactly what she'd been silently begging for.

He filled her, stretching her, as her body accepted his invasion. She arched back, grinding her hips down into him in an effort to get every inch of his body into her own.

She could feel him high inside her, the heat and heft

of him. Her muscles clenched him as he pulled back out, trying to keep him where she wanted him most.

In no time he returned, with slow, smooth strokes that sent her closer and closer to the edge.

It wasn't long—seconds, minutes, she had no idea— before she was breaking apart into pieces around him. The world, the pressure and pleasure converged on her in a way that stole every bit of consciousness and coherency from her.

She had no idea what had happened. One minute she was riding the crest of the best orgasm in her life and the next she was lying on the floor beside him.

She had to take stock, actually cataloging the feel of his arm lodged beneath her body at an awkward angle from shoulder to hip. The way one of her legs was thrown over his in a wanton sprawl.

She'd never blacked out in her life, but she thought that maybe it was something like this. Losing seconds or minutes and wondering what the hell you had missed.

The tremors of aftershocks that rocked her body were evidence that she'd more than enjoyed the black hole in her memory.

Her heart still raced, stuttering and protesting as it found a slower rhythm. Beneath the arch of her shoulder, she could feel the answering beat of Luke's heart against her back.

"Well." His single word brushed the curved edge of her cheek, fluttering damp tendrils of hair and making the muscles of her sex convulse in yet another tremor.

As nondescript as the word had been she thought it probably said everything. "Well."

Several minutes of silence stretched between them, their panting breaths the only sound. "If this doesn't remind me of my misspent youth I don't know what would."

Ainsley rolled her head against the floor to look at him, not having the energy to do more than that at the moment. "What do you mean?"

"I mean, thank God Gran didn't walk in during the middle of *that*." She could hear the self-deprecating amusement that laced his words.

"What's that saying about small favors?"

Chuckling, Luke rolled onto his side, pillowing her body in the crook of his shoulder. Her muscles protested their rough use and the hard surface beneath them, but she didn't move. She didn't want to be anywhere but cradled in Luke's arms.

Propping his head up on his hand, he stared down at her. She could barely hold her eyes open, thanks to a combination of emotional upheaval and earth-shattering orgasm. Unfortunately, Luke didn't look sleepy at all.

In fact, he looked rather contemplative as his gaze roamed her face. She wondered what he was thinking but figured he would tell her when he was ready. Prying had never gotten her anywhere with this man. Despite what they'd just shared, she had no reason to think it would work tonight.

She'd just close her eyes for a moment while she waited.

The world tilted. Somewhere in her subconscious she registered the change in her position. However, even as her brain told her she was off balance, her instincts told her she was perfectly safe.

Her eyes fluttered reluctantly open anyway.

"You're fine. I've got you." His words, the warm timbre of his voice, his strong arms around her—she really did feel safe snuggled against him.

Her eyes shut again as she burrowed closer. She knew from the feel of his body against hers that he carried her up the stairs and laid her gently in the center of his bed.

Curling beside her, he maneuvered them together so that her back was tucked into the protective curve of his chest. He slung an arm over her waist, his fingers gently curled around the swell of her breast. A tingle, a muted reminder of what she'd felt earlier, rushed through her at the touch. But there was no demand, no expectation in the contact. Rather, it was a connection—his body to hers.

With a sigh of satisfaction that had nothing to do with her physical fulfillment, she feel asleep again, knowing that when she woke he would still be right beside her.

AINSLEY CREPT DOWN THE vacant hallway to the sanctuary of her office. Early-morning light streamed through the windows, taking the chill from the air. She'd strategically placed the desk chair in the best spot of sunshine. It was one of her pleasures, to sit here in the quiet morning soaking up the warmth like a cat.

However, today she didn't have time for that.

She wanted to get through her work early because she had no idea what the rest of the day might hold.

Her body ached in the most satisfying way. She wanted to spend the rest of the day with Luke. Laughing. Loving. Or simply sharing her happiness with him.

However, that bubbling euphoria was severely dampened when she saw the reminder note waiting for her on the computer keyboard. She'd forgotten all about Luke's financial paperwork.

For the sale of the orchard.

She was an idiot. No, that wasn't precisely true. She was a romantic fool who'd let her body overrule her mind once again. She could build all the castles in the sky she wanted, it wasn't going to change the fact that this time with Luke was fleeting.

He'd be gone before the ink on the sale documents could dry.

Sitting alongside the sticky note were the college applications that she'd been avoiding for weeks. No more. It was time to face the truth and put her plan into action.

It took her an hour to complete three of the applications. Stamping and addressing their envelopes, she set them to the side and changed her focus.

Half an hour later, she finished pulling together the financial reports Luke had asked for. It made her slightly upset to look at them…to see what she and his grandparents had done over the past eight years, what he was throwing away. They were profitable. Actually, they were a successful enterprise. Agriculture wasn't exactly the easiest way to earn a living, but they'd made it work for them. They'd spent years building a reputation for high quality.

None of that mattered to Luke. Two days ago she'd told herself she didn't care what he did.

Today she had to admit she'd lied. Then and now. She did care. She didn't want to see him give up a heritage that one day he'd miss. She didn't want to see him make a decision he'd regret.

But there was nothing she could do about it. She held no delusions about what was going to happen. As much as last night had meant to her—and, she hoped, to him—he wouldn't change the course that he'd set. He was selling, leaving.

Sadness coursed through her as she closed the program and reached for the pages spitting out onto the printer beside her.

Stacking them together and grabbing the envelopes, she headed for the kitchen. In her current mood she wasn't sure if she wanted to see him there or not.

It turned out, she didn't have to decide. Instead of Luke, Gran sat in the kitchen. She stared out the window at the orchard. Her eyes held a faraway sadness that compounded Ainsley's own melancholy.

"Gran?"

She turned to take Ainsley in, a motion that seemed to take much longer than it should. As if, while she wanted to participate in the world around her, the temptation to sit there staring out that window and ignoring everything was too great.

"Ainsley. Good morning. I'm sorry I didn't make coffee…" She trailed off, leaving the end of her statement *but I didn't feel like doing it* unsaid. That was so unlike the Gran she'd always known.

"Don't worry about it. I'll take care of it."

Dropping the papers onto the counter, Ainsley noticed another stack sitting in a neat pile at the far edge.

She stepped over, a quick glance telling her they were Luke's. For the Realtor. She added hers to the top, knowing that when he finally did come down he'd see them immediately.

With a snap in her step, she returned to the main counter area and quickly pulled together a breakfast of pumpkin spice muffins and coffee.

Sitting down across from Gran, Ainsley was happy to see her eyes more focused. That faraway look scared her. She was afraid that one day Gran just wouldn't come back.

"Gran? I have to run into town. Can you tell Luke that I've left the information he needed with his papers? He asked me to email them to the Realtor but he didn't leave me her address."

Gran nodded, the ghost of a smile flitting across her lips. "Certainly, dear."

Ainsley narrowed her eyes, but Gran definitely seemed more coherent. She'd follow up later but right now she needed to get to town and back. Preferably before Luke realized she was gone.

Dropping her applications into the mailbox had somehow become the most important task in her day. However, while she was out, and if he was hell-bent on selling, perhaps she could have some influence over who ended up with the property.

12

LUKE STIRRED IN BED, reaching out even half-asleep and searching the covers beside him. For what? Who?

His eyes popped open. Ainsley.

Who wasn't there.

Her side of the bed was rumpled. However, the entire bed looked as if a tornado had passed over it, twisting the covers into a lump. It certainly hadn't bothered him last night.

He'd had one need last night. Ainsley. He'd been consumed with the desire to imprint his body and soul onto every square inch of her skin, to leave no doubt that she was his.

And despite everything, he wanted to do it again. Right now. Which made him a little grumpy as he rolled from the bed alone.

Where was she?

Throwing on the first clothes he could find, he headed down the hallway to her room. It, too, was empty, the bed undisturbed.

That soothed the anxious sensation that churned in his stomach. At least she hadn't slipped from his bed to her own sometime in the wee hours of the morning. That idea did not sit well with him—that while he was apparently becoming more and more obsessed with her, she could dismiss him so easily.

No, the authoritative businessman he'd become took issue with the loss of control and power in that scenario.

However, apparently that was not what had happened so…

He backtracked down the hallway and headed to the main floor.

He could hear sounds in the kitchen so that's where he looked first, a smile of anticipation spreading across his face.

Finding Gran at the sink was not what he'd expected. As much as it helped to see her doing the mundane chore she'd handled every night during his childhood, she wasn't Ainsley.

"Morning, Gran."

She turned to look at him, a smile lifting up one corner of her mouth, as if she didn't have the emotions to fully back it up.

"Luke. Would you like some breakfast, dear?"

"No, no. I'll just grab a cup of coffee." He reached for a mug and poured from the pot on the counter. Turning to lean against the worn Formica counter, he crossed his arms and took his first hot, invigorating sip.

"Have you seen Ainsley?"

"Yes, dear." Reaching over, Gran patted his arm with a still-damp hand, leaving four thin strips of water against the dark gray of his shirt. "As a matter of fact, she asked me to let you know she emailed those numbers to the Realtor before she went into town."

He let that sink in for a second. She'd been busy this morning. "Do you know where she was going?"

"She didn't say."

"I wish she'd waited for me. I have to run into town later. We could have gone together." With a shrug, Luke turned to press a quick kiss to Gran's papery thin cheek. "I'm going to go call into the office first, though. Is there anything I can do for you?"

"Not a thing." This time when she smiled up at him the expression seemed a little easier, a little fuller. "You're a good boy, Luke."

While her compliment warmed him from the inside out, it also made him slightly uneasy—Gran seemed to be living in her own world lately, and he wondered if he was missing something important.

GRAN OPENED THE DOOR beneath the sink, pulling the trash can out on the little runners Ainsley had installed for them several years ago. She was such a sweet girl. Always finding ways to help, to make life easier.

It broke Gran's heart to see her so sad after everything she'd been through. If there was a girl who deserved a little happiness, it was Ainsley. Gran understood the pain of losing a child too early... But she'd had her Brian to get her through. Ainsley had no one.

No one except Luke.

They were so perfect together. How could they not see?

Shaking her head, Gran picked up the last plate from breakfast and scraped the remains of her picked-apart muffin into the trash…on top of the papers Ainsley had prepared for Luke's Realtor.

Some people just needed a little help.

AINSLEY RETURNED FROM running errands and posting her applications to find Luke gone. He wasn't in the house and she didn't figure that he'd gone outside to wander the orchard alone. Every time he'd wanted to see the farm he'd taken her with him—he needed her expertise. So she assumed he'd also headed into town on some errand.

The house was quiet. Too quiet after days of tension— both sexual and antagonistic—between them. She almost missed the charged energy now that he was gone.

She poked her head into Gran's room only to discover that she was taking a nap.

Going back downstairs to the office, she settled into the business of running the orchard. While she was honored to do it, the time she'd spent making arrangements for Pops had put her severely behind on the day-to-day operation of running a business.

She'd just gotten started when a loud knock on the front door startled her. They almost never had visitors, not to the farmhouse anyway.

Opening the door, she studied the three people standing on her front porch. Mr. and Mrs. Kincaid, a couple that she knew rather well because they owned a peach farm in the area. And a tall woman with a slick blond bob, blood-red fingernails and a tailored gray pantsuit that most certainly did not belong on the farm.

Ainsley focused on the woman. "Can I help you?"

"We're meeting Mr. Collier."

"I'm sorry, he's not here right now."

The frown that puckered the blonde's lips didn't even budge the smooth plane of her forehead. "But we have an appointment to view the farm."

Suddenly the pieces all fell into place. She should have realized immediately. Ainsley turned her gaze to the Kincaids and smiled. If someone had to purchase the property they were as good as any. She knew they could handle the orchard, would probably keep their workers on and wouldn't mind if Ainsley wanted to stop by and visit every now and then.

The question, though, was where was Luke? It was totally out of character for him to miss something like this. While he hadn't needed to use his phone often since he'd been here, she'd heard his BlackBerry calendar beep at him off and on, reminding him of responsibilities back home that he would miss.

He had the technology and wasn't afraid to use it to keep his schedule in line. And even if he ultimately ignored the reminder, he always glanced at the screen to make sure it was something he could dismiss.

She had two choices. Tell them they'd need to reschedule, or conduct the walk-through herself. She was probably the best person to show them around anyway.

Luke was still learning the finer details of running the orchard.

Joining the trio on the porch, Ainsley did what her conscience dictated. "I'll tell you what, why don't I show you around? Luke's probably just running later in town than he expected."

The experience was bittersweet. On one hand, she enjoyed showing off what they'd built here, especially to fellow farmers who would appreciate the changes and upgrades they'd made. But on the other hand, she was showing what had become her home to someone else who wanted to own it. The orchard was a piece of her life that she wasn't ready to give up. Admitting that was difficult because there was nothing she could do to change the situation.

She'd always tackled problems head-on. This was one that had no visible solution. She didn't like the loss of control.

"We've upgraded a lot of the equipment over the past few years. Most everything is current. We have six employees on staff year-round and of course we hire seasonal workers for thinning and picking."

Mr. Kincaid stopped at the packing shed and watched as they prepared the harvest for shipment to the client. She could tell as he inspected their equipment, the procedures and their workers, that he knew what he was doing. But then she'd already known that.

He asked her several questions, including some about the current staff. "Have you asked them if they're willing to stay?"

She looked at him and knew that she had to be completely honest. "Until I opened the door, I didn't realize who the interested buyers were, Fred. If I'd known I might have asked, but I'm not involved in the actual sale."

The pity that crossed his face almost made her angry. "I'm sorry this is happening, Ainsley. Everyone wishes Brian had left the farm to you."

In everything that had happened, in all the times she'd wished things could be different, owning the orchard had never been her desire. "I don't, Fred, but I appreciate the thought. The farm belongs with a Collier, and I'm not part of the family."

"The hell you aren't."

She'd never heard the other man, soft-spoken and particular, use that kind of language before. He was a throwback to a generation where men simply didn't swear in the presence of a lady.

She smiled, and said, "Thanks. But this is the way things needed to be. If you buy, I'll be glad to know the farm's in good hands."

"Could I convince you to stay on?"

It was a possibility she hadn't even considered. However, it didn't take her long to know what her answer would be. "Thank you, but no. It's time for me to move on, too." There were too many memories here.

She couldn't stay. Not this time. Not without Luke.

They finished their tour back at the front porch of the house. She offered them a glass of lemonade but they declined. They'd already seen the house many times over the years, and didn't really care about the home anyway. The Kincaids were interested in the trees.

Ainsley waved goodbye as they drove away.

Luke's red Jag, the shiny paint dulled by a thin coat of dust, sat in the driveway again. Wherever he'd gone, he was now back.

And he hadn't bothered to come and find her.

A frown playing around her lips, she turned into the house to find him but got only as far as the study. She could hear him behind the closed door, the timbre of his voice and the escalating tightness of his tone suggesting that whomever he was talking to, Luke was not happy.

She thought about interrupting him for a second but changed her mind when his words blasted through the door.

"Damn it!"

She backed away, deciding there was plenty of time to tell him that he'd missed a meeting with a potential buyer. It sounded as if he had enough problems to deal with for now.

He finally appeared in the kitchen just as they were finishing dinner preparations; his pinched face and shuttered eyes confirmed her suspicions. Half of her wanted to ask, wanted to offer him an ear for whatever the problem was. The other half secretly hoped it had something to do with the sale of the orchard.

However, she wasn't holding her breath.

She settled for "Is everything okay?"

He glanced at her for the first time since he'd entered the room and it was amazing. She watched as the gathering cloud of his frustration and anger melted away, like sugar into hot water.

He crossed to her, laid his palm against the small of her back and leaned down to press his lips to hers in a soft kiss.

She was startled and a little embarrassed—Gran sat not three feet away at the table. Luke pulled back, looking down into her face with the same sweet smile on his lips and said, "Fine now."

Ainsley's heart kicked beneath her ribs.

Turning back to the simmering pot on the stove, she smiled over her shoulder at him. "Glad I could help." But beneath the surface, countless emotions bubbled just as fiercely as the food she was cooking.

He was sending her mixed signals and she did not have the experience to handle them. Not from Luke.

She glanced at Gran to gauge her reaction. But the older woman seemed to be unaware of what was happening right in front of her, her eyes focused on something only she could see.

"Oh, the Kincaids and your Realtor stopped by this afternoon to tour the orchard."

"What?" Luke stopped halfway to sitting down in his seat at the table. If she hadn't been so surprised at the shocked expression on his face, the way his body was half-folded in on itself, suspended in midair, might have been humorous. Her stomach tightened with apprehension instead.

"They said they had an appointment with you today. You were in town so I showed them around."

Storm clouds gathered in his eyes once again, turning the bright green to a tumultuous green-gray. He dropped into the waiting chair, the wood rocking back with the force of his descent.

"Damn it," he muttered, sounding more irritated than outraged this time.

"Thanks for covering for me. Her message must have gotten lost in the shuffle. At least I hope that's what happened." His hands bracketed his face, his fingers massaging from his temples to the bridge of his nose. He folded his hands over his face, but his muffled words were still audible. "Ever have one of those days? Nothing seems to be going right."

She resisted the urge to reach for him, to lay her hand across his and tell him everything would be okay. Instead she offered him a chance to share the burden of his bad day. "Anything I can do to help?"

Lifting his fingers from his face, he looked at her from between his open palms. "No."

That was it. No explanation. No thanks for the offer. Nothing else. Just a simple, concise, no-wiggle-room no.

She'd slept in his bed twice now. In less than a week she'd gone from being lonely to sharing her life with Luke. Again. Whether she'd planned on it or not.

They shared a house, a breakfast table and a bed. What they didn't share was anything important. That bothered her more than she was ready to admit, because admitting it meant she wanted more from him. More from their reunion than she had any right to expect.

Unfortunately, she couldn't seem to stop herself from wanting it anyway.

As she sat down across from Luke and watched him wolf down the food she'd prepared, Ainsley could see herself doing this every night for the rest of her life. Eight years ago, she would have been content with that. With simply being in the sphere of Luke's world.

Now she realized there was so much more. Luke's ability to keep pieces of himself hidden and protected scared her and mystified her at the same time. She didn't know how to do that. She felt everything, did everything and experienced everything to the fullest degree.

While he was constantly holding back.

The fact that she was in for a huge dose of heartache went without saying. She accepted it as a done deal. But even that couldn't convince her to experience these moments with him with anything less than the full measure of her heart and soul.

Their time together might be brief but at least she'd have some vivid memories to survive on when he was gone.

As usual, they cleared the kitchen and waited for Gran to head upstairs to her own room. It was early, around nine o'clock, but Ainsley was gratified by the way Luke grabbed her the minute his grandmother was gone. The evidence of the consuming arousal she inspired in him was comforting.

He crushed his mouth to hers, whispering, "I missed you today. I don't like waking up alone when I expect to find you there."

She laughed. A sound that broke directly in the center when he ran his teeth across the curve of her neck. He knew exactly where to touch her.

Was that a good or a bad thing? She wasn't certain. She supposed it depended on whether or not his knowledge of her body's weaknesses reflected an understanding of her emotional weaknesses. And whether or not he could exploit the widening chinks in her armor to hurt her again.

He reached for her, his eyes smoldering. She could see the consuming desire there and realized if she didn't get him someplace private they were going to end up having sex on the kitchen table.

There were so many reasons *that* was a bad idea, starting with his grandmother.

Stiffening her elbows she pushed him back, a half smile curving her lips. "Not here."

His eyes narrowed as he studied her for several seconds. She had no doubt he was gauging her resolve and calculating whether or not he could sway her to his way of thinking. Apparently, deciding he couldn't, he swept her up into his arms and crushed her against his chest. A startled squeal burst from her lips and her hands grabbed tight to his shoulders.

He strode through the house, stopping long enough for her to reach across his body to flip off the kitchen light. Darkness surrounded them as he made his way to her office.

"You really have to stop doing this."

"Doing what?"

"Carrying me around." What was this, two, no three times? She couldn't keep the happiness that tinged her words from coming through.

"Maybe I like it."

She reached for the hem of her shirt, pulling it over her head, and popped open the fastening to her front-clasp bra quickly after. She'd worn it today wondering if the easy access would come in handy. It had.

His steps faltered as his gaze refocused on her bared breasts. A seductive smile tugged at her lips.

She felt powerful. Sexy. Feminine. Only he had ever made her feel that way.

He reached back with a foot and kicked the door closed behind them. Walking the small pathway to the desk, he plopped her rear onto the pile of papers sitting there.

She opened her mouth to protest—some of these were pretty darn important—but he cut her off.

"I'm not taking my hands off you long enough to lock that damn door. If Gran comes in here without knocking then she deserves to get an eyeful."

His mouth latched onto her neck and her body arched up into the moist heat of his kiss. His hands brushed down her skin, cupping the swell of her breasts. The heat of him seeped into her, puckering her nipples to tight buds. His palms circled over them in a teasing gesture that wasn't nearly enough pressure for what she wanted.

"That wasn't what I was going to say." Her words stuttered as he bent to dip his tongue beneath the shield of his fingers.

"Oh?"

She rocked back onto her hips, deliberately rustling the papers beneath her.

He glanced at the papers. "Well, there wasn't a lot of choice given the lack of open space in here." His teeth grazed over the tendon from the curve of her shoulder up to her throat. A shiver of longing shook down her spine.

"Luke."

With a sigh of frustration, he pulled back from her, reaching for the computer monitor sitting on the corner of the desk.

But he wasn't reaching to move it, in fact the flat of his palm connected with the side of the casing as if he was ready to shove it off the desk and shatter it into a million pieces.

"Don't you dare!"

"I'll buy you a new one. The thing is practically a dinosaur. It needs to be put out of its misery."

"You do that and the only thing you'll be touching tonight is broken glass."

He laughed, a sound that settled somewhere in the center of her chest, spreading and warming her from the inside out.

"Fine."

She expected him to grasp her hand and drag her from the room to another private place. Instead, he took a step back, reaching for the hem of his shirt as he did. It was over his head and swinging from the corner of a crate in seconds. Fishing a condom from his pocket, he laid it on the desk, the heat and scent of him drifting over her as he came close once more. She wanted to reach for him but didn't…she was more intrigued right now with what he might do next.

His fingers worked the fly of his jeans. The rasp of the zipper sent a flood of anticipation pouring down her spine. His jeans dropped to the floor and he kicked them away, the denim making a loud *thwack* when they connected with the underside of her desk.

The view she would get when he had to crawl back under there to retrieve them was going to be sensational. She almost asked him to turn around so she could get a preview, but decided some things were worth the wait.

He stood before her, beautiful. Well made and perfectly masculine.

His hands bracketing her rib cage, Luke lifted her from the desk, setting her down on the floor before him. "Your turn."

His eyes stayed on her…waiting. She watched the rise and fall of his chest, the rapid pulse at the base of his throat, clear signs of his anticipation and arousal. If she'd needed anything other than his enticing erection.

He kept moving away until the backs of his knees collided with the seat of her office chair and he collapsed onto the waiting cushion. His eyes were level with the low waist of her shorts, the perfect height for what she had yet to reveal.

It was her turn to slowly work the zipper, to peel back each layer of cloth that covered her sex, that kept her from him. She was the one doing the opening but his eyes said he was the one receiving the present.

With a roll of her hips, she pushed the clinging material, shorts and panties, until they slid silently down her legs. Lifting one foot out of the pool of cloth, she spread her legs wide, showing him everything.

In a burst of movement, Luke shot the chair across the floor. His arms wrapped around her body, crushing her to him. He buried his face in the naked expanse of her stomach. She felt the tickle of his breath cross her skin as he exhaled slowly. His tongue followed, a warm, wet caress that swirled at the curves of her belly button.

He pushed her backward, keeping her hips prisoner with one arm even as he urged her off balance. She had nowhere to go except against the unforgiving desk. Papers spilled over as her hands wrapped around the edges, grasping for something to anchor her to reality.

She no longer cared about making a mess. She'd have plenty of time to sort it out tomorrow.

Her arched back thrust her hips forward and opened her body to him. She was standing and he was practically prostrate at her feet, yet she felt the prisoner here, held to this spot by the promise in his gaze as he looked up from the open V of her thighs.

She was afraid her own eyes held a desperation she really didn't want to admit to. But he left her no choice. This she couldn't hide from him. She was an ache that only he could soothe.

His mouth curved up into a wicked grin right before it touched down on the lips of her sex. She could smell her own arousal, heady and thick between them. His tongue darted out, warm and wet. He speared close to the heat of her but didn't go nearly far enough to satisfy.

He used the moist heat of his breath to tease as he pulled back. Her body contracted on the need for his touch, and a shudder passed through her.

Luke came back for more, this time running his tongue from the base of her sex to the very top. Her body bowed up and her eyes slid shut when he hit the sweet spot, flicking her clit with the tip of his tongue.

He spread her wider and went in for more. A growl of satisfaction vibrated through the back of his throat and into her. She could feel it through the conductor of his tongue as he thrust it deep inside.

There was no gentle nibbling, no teasing, no polite foray. They were both too far gone for that. He laved her with the flat of his tongue, as if he could take in all of her with this one act…this one caress.

She writhed beneath him, caught between the edge of pleasure and the awareness that it wasn't enough. Not nearly enough. She wanted more.…

He slipped a finger inside her, pulling a gasp from deep in her chest.

She couldn't help watching him as he knelt at her feet. The expression on his face—one of complete enthrallment—was as arousing as his touch.

She watched as the tip of his tongue found her clit again, and a jolt of pleasure shot through her core. Somewhere in the back of her cloudy mind she heard the squeak of the chair as it rolled closer and the soles of her feet were propped against the back. Her fingers fisted around the desk, holding tight to the only thing keeping her anchored.

A whimper ground out of the back of her throat just as the world began to explode around her. Her body bucked violently against Luke as she reached the peak, and he wrapped one arm around her waist to keep her from falling off the desk.

Her entire focus, her entire being, was centered where he touched her. Nothing else existed.

But even as her body began to settle, her lungs deciding maybe they could work again after all, he pulled her to him. She glided bonelessly from the desk into his lap. Her legs slid perfectly between the wide oval of the arms so that she was straddling him.

The heat of him was startling. His skin burned.

She'd barely recovered from one unimaginable orgasm and suddenly she craved another. Grabbing handfuls of his hair, she dragged his mouth to hers tasting her own satisfaction on his tongue. She poured every ounce of desire into the kiss, arching her body, touching him, letting him know that she wanted more.

She nipped at his neck, tasting salt and sun and Luke. She could hear the rustle of papers as he fumbled behind her and the loud tear as he opened the foil packet. She rolled her hips against him, caressing his erection and enjoying the way his eyes glazed and his hand dangled, condom forgotten for a moment.

Reaching between them she brought her hand into the mix, grasping him in her tight fist. She wanted to feel the smoothness of the skin that covered his sex, to know the pulse of blood that ran beneath the surface. To touch the evidence of his desire for her without the shield of latex between them. Part of her wanted the feel of only him deep inside her even as she knew that, considering their history, that was probably the dumbest idea she'd ever had.

Instead, she took the condom from his fingers. His eyes glittered and his breath panted in and out as he watched her roll it down his length.

Fisting him again, she guided the head of his cock to the opening of her body. She could feel the slick moisture from her orgasm and the echoing pulse of it even as he pushed partway inside.

Rearing back, she arched her hips and took all of him that she could take. Her body contracted around him, enjoying the weight deep inside. He was perfect, hot and heavy and she could feel him filling her up.

His fingers dug into the curve of her hips, holding her still against the increasing need to drive them both on. The ache built again, sharp and surprising because she'd just come. This time there was more. She could feel the tingling energy left from her first orgasm as it shot through the walls of her sex. She spasmed around him, her body primed by the memory of what he'd already given her and the knowledge that she could have more.

As if he'd been waiting for a sign, he began to move them both. His hips rocked hard against her as the cage of his hands lifted her and brought her back again. Her feet found purchase on the rolling undercarriage of the chair, giving her leverage. Her thighs flexed in time to his rhythm as tension built deep inside.

The climb was steeper but the payoff greater as her body exploded for the second time. Tears slipped beneath her closed lashes. Her fingers curved into the arch of his shoulders, her nails digging into skin and grabbing hold of him as the only stable thing in her chaotic universe.

He bucked beneath her, a cry of pleasure bursting from his lips as he pumped his own release into her. He held on to her, too, leaving bruises on her hips that she'd gladly wear tomorrow.

She collapsed onto him, and they both let the chair take the deadweight of their temporarily useless bodies. His skin was warm and damp against her. She shouldn't have liked that but she did.

Her head settled into the crook of his neck and she inhaled deeply, enjoying the scent of their shared pleasure as it settled around them. His arms came to rest around her hips, the only motion he could seem to manage was to tighten those muscles and pull her even closer against him.

They stayed that way, for minutes, a half hour, she wasn't certain. It didn't matter. They were both content and sated and for the moment that was enough.

Finally her muscles began to stiffen and protest their unusual position. Wiggling against him, she placed her palms to the desk behind them and pushed herself up out of their awkward hold.

She sat on the edge of the desk again. This time as she looked down on him, rumpled and flushed with a pleasure that still coursed through her body, she didn't care what came next.

With a smile she said, "I could get used to this."

In the morning she'd probably regret the honesty of that statement, but for now, it was the truth and she'd kept enough secrets from him.

13

THEIR DAYS FELL INTO a pattern. Ainsley would wake before Luke, getting out of bed at the crack of dawn to attend to the business of harvesting peaches. He'd wake up…sometime. She was never sure when, but whenever she came back to the house for a quick lunch and a chance to cool off he was there. Waiting for her.

Often they'd share the brief snatch of time with Gran. Sometimes they'd be alone. They never talked about anything important; this time was just to be and enjoy.

She knew that he was having some trouble with a potential client he'd been working with before he arrived here. He never told her specifics but she knew the negotiations weren't going well. At night she'd find him in the study, his hair almost standing on end as if he'd fought the urge to pull it out…just.

She'd asked him about it once but he'd dismissed her offer of a sympathetic ear. She hadn't offered again.

Their nights were filled with passion, connection and, for her, blossoming hope. She knew she shouldn't let it take hold, but she did. She couldn't stop it any more than she could stop her heart from beating.

There were other signs, signs against the idyllic fantasy she was building around the affair. Things were clearly proceeding on the sale of the orchard.

In the end, Luke had received three competing offers from neighboring farmers who wanted to purchase the land. As far as she was aware, the Kincaids had made the winning bid. The details were complicated, turning over the property in the middle of a harvest with an active contract. They were just waiting for the client to sign papers agreeing to the change in ownership so that the sale could proceed before the contract was fulfilled. They didn't anticipate any problems as Fred Kincaid had already agreed in writing to fulfill the obligation. It was a formality. One that was holding everything up.

Ainsley didn't mind. The longer it took, the more time she had with Luke.

There had been a few glitches along the way, lost paperwork, unconnected phone calls. Luke's missed appointment with the Kincaids.

So far, it had been nothing major, just small things that niggled in the back of her mind. And Luke's, too. On more than one occasion he'd blown his top over these minor setbacks.

His frustration hurt. It was proof that he wanted to get out of here. Away from her. The problem was that she could never see that when they were together.

When they were together she felt like the center of his world.

She was getting tired of walking the tightrope, though. During the day she was bombarded with reasons and reminders to pull away. At night she was swept off her feet by his passion and her own desire, unable to heed the warnings she gave herself when the sun was out.

Her own plans were proceeding, as well. Just this afternoon, she'd received an acceptance letter to Auburn's agricultural program. She had several hours toward an accounting degree, which would only enhance her ability to succeed now that she'd found her true calling. She loved farm life and wanted to be able to use the skills that she'd learned here at Collier Orchards.

So why was she suddenly uncertain about what she should really do?

WHEN DINNER WAS OVER, the kitchen cleaned and Gran ensconced firmly in her own room, they began their nightly routine. Ainsley and Luke would take different sides of the house, make sure everything was secure, meet at the bottom of the stairs and kiss their way to the top.

Tonight, things would be different. Tonight, he had a surprise.

Grasping her hand, instead of bringing her closer he tugged her sideways toward the door.

"What are you doing?"

"I have something I want to show you. A surprise."

He watched with fascination as she raised her eyebrows, her widened eyes full of wary reluctance.

She didn't like surprises, something he'd never known

about her. He wondered if this was new or if she'd always been that way. He thought back over their relationship and couldn't think of a single time where he'd thought to surprise her.

He really had been a prick, hadn't he?

Her reluctant feet trudged down the hallway behind him. The weight of her body pulled against his hand and tried to slow his progress. Turning around, he let her collide with him, wrapping his arms around her and pinning her to his chest.

Reaching down with his lips, he coaxed her into a state of melted awareness with nothing more than his mouth and tongue. But he refused to get sidetracked. Not tonight. It was too important.

Pulling back, he whispered, "Trust me," before heading for the door. This time her steps weren't so much reluctant as unaware.

Until they rounded the first bend in the path outside, where one of the four-wheelers waited. Her demeanor quickly changed. She let go of his hand and shot forward, anger replacing the wary reluctance she'd been harboring before.

"What is this doing here? Everyone knows not to leave them out at night."

"I told them to."

She turned puzzled eyes back to him. "Why would you do that?"

"Because we need it." Throwing a leg over, he turned the machine on, reveling in the loud hum and vibrating power beneath him. The energy seemed to course directly from the machine to his body, increasing his already-purring anticipation for what was to come. "Get on."

She sat behind him, grasping his hips in a loose hold that wouldn't do at all. Reaching behind him, he took both of her arms, wrapped them tightly around his waist and enjoyed the way her body had to drape across his. He could feel the thrust of her breasts against his back and his mouth began to water for the taste of them on his tongue.

But he could wait. He'd have to.

If he tortured himself by taking the curves a little faster and a little sharper just to feel her rubbing against him...well, he was only human.

From the tiny gasps he felt brushing against his neck, he wasn't the only one affected by the friction.

When they pulled up to his destination, she slid from behind him.

"The pond? You want to take a late-night swim?"

"Eventually. I thought the water might come in handy."

She looked up at him, completely bewildered. "For what?"

Once again taking her hand, he led her into the first line of trees to a blanket he'd set up there just before it got dark. There was a gleaming silver ice bucket, empty. Next to it sat a small cooler, not exactly romantic in appearance but definitely practical. Inside he knew she'd find a chilled bottle of wine, some cheese, crackers and a tray of fruit with several of their own peaches, fresh from the tree as its centerpiece. He'd asked Mitch for a few of the best that had been picked today.

At strategic intervals around the blanket sat several small votive candles just waiting to be lit.

She turned to him, her eyes wide. They glittered with happiness, desire and something that made the center of his chest ache. Disbelief that he'd gone to so much trouble for *her*.

"I suppose I should be grateful you didn't light those ahead of time," she said playfully as she took in the scene one more time.

"I might be oblivious sometimes, but I'm not that stupid."

"Thank heaven for small favors." While she was clearly teasing him, the bursting smile on her lips said everything he needed to hear.

This surprise, at least, had been good. He helped her settle down on the blanket before fiddling with the spread.

Placing the tray between them, he handed her a glass of the sweet white wine and told her, "Stretch out and relax."

"Easy for you to say."

"No, no it really isn't."

Their drive was something they had in common. They seemed to share this need to keep their hands and minds busy. However, he had learned over the past several years that taking time out was necessary every now and then. And taking time out with Ainsley was a luxury he'd never pass up.

Doing as he asked, she stretched her legs before her, propped her head on one hand and raised an eyebrow as if to ask *what next?*

He picked up a slice of cheese and held it to her lips, waiting for them to part. When she leaned forward to take the bite he offered, the edge of her tongue licked across his skin. Her teeth bit down, nearly nipping the tip of his finger before he quickly pulled it away. The seductive smile on her lips told him that had been no accident.

She reached for a piece herself, but before she could touch it he stopped her hand, shaking his head. "This is for you."

Although, that was a lie. Watching bliss cross her face was a treat he'd never thought to have again.

Grabbing a strawberry, he rubbed it across her lips staining them a deep, dark pink with the juices before pushing the berry inside her waiting mouth. He watched the column of her throat as she tipped back her head to swallow a mouthful of wine. Her skin was soft and dusky. Inviting. The urge to reach in and take a bite of her was overwhelming, but he wasn't finished with this seduction yet.

Instead, he contented himself with reaching forward to lick the line of her still-parted lips. He took the juice he'd left behind but no more.

Smacking his own lips he said, "Sweet."

He pulled away and she followed, reaching out to force him back. Grasping her hands in a fist, again he shook his head. "No, ma'am."

Her eyes flashed, combat, desire, a promise of retaliation. He knew he'd enjoy that just as much as he was enjoying this.

This time he selected a slice of peach from the tray. The flesh was cool to the touch and a beautiful pale orange color. The juices rolled over his fingers just from picking it up. They really did grow the best peaches in all of Georgia.

This time he held the fruit to her mouth, waiting for her to take a bite of what he offered. She gobbled up half of the slice in the first bite. A single drop of nectar glistened at the corner of her lips. Leaning forward, he licked it away before offering her the last morsel.

Just as she moved closer to accept, he dropped it...directly into the open V of her shirt. A hiss pushed through her teeth but she didn't move. He'd half expected a squeal, but not from his Ainsley. She knew exactly what he was doing and wanted him to do it.

"Oops." He smiled at her with an impish grin, confirming it had been no accident.

Leaning forward, he pulled the edges of her shirt back, letting his warm breath brush across her skin. "I suppose you shouldn't be the only one enjoying the fruit. It does look really good."

Dipping his mouth to the rounded flesh of her breast, he licked the trail of sticky moisture the peach had left there before finding and eating the small piece.

"I think I've ruined your shirt. Better take it off."

He waited as she watched him, deciding whether to comply or balk. When she reached for the hem, crossing her arms and lifting it off of her body in one smooth motion, he smiled. She was naked beneath, her breasts swaying free before him.

"You." She gestured with a finger, making sure he knew exactly what she meant. With a shrug, he pulled his own shirt over his head. It was no more than he wanted anyway. To be naked with her beneath the trees and the stars.

He reached for another piece of fruit, this time a section of orange, offering her the first bite before taking the rest himself. He swore he could taste her there on his tongue, her sweetness mingling with the burst of juices.

This time the juice dribbled slowly down his chin, impeded by his stubble. Ainsley scooted closer, imprisoning her own hands beneath her legs and leaning forward to lick. She grazed the side of his face, to the crease of his lips, the sharp little tip of her tongue spearing inside to swipe at his own.

Before she could take more, he reached for a strawberry and trailed it down the side of her neck, over her shoulder, swirling it across the tip of her breast. It left a shiny pink trail over her skin, a clear path for him to follow in case he got lost in the wonders of her body.

He enjoyed the sharp intake of her breath at the touch of the chilled fruit to her heated skin. Popping it into his mouth, he touched his lips to the trail and followed it, not with his tongue but with little love bites. At perfect intervals the pale pink turned to a sharp red where he nipped and sucked at her skin. She leaned toward him, urging him on.

When he finally sucked the tight point of her nipple into the heat of his mouth she let out a low-throated moan and threw her head back with an abandon that floored him. One simple touch, a few precious minutes and she was surrendering herself to him body and soul.

The trust she held in him was awe-inspiring and downright scary. He'd never, in his entire life, trusted another person so completely, the way that she trusted him.

And it wasn't just this moment. It was everything she did, the way she approached life. If anyone in the world had a reason to doubt others it was Ainsley. She'd grown up with the person who should have protected her hurting her most. Anyone else would have locked herself away, would have kept others at a distance, to avoid ever having to experience that pain again.

Not Ainsley. She offered her whole self to everything and everyone around her. She was open and giving and always had been. Luke wondered how he could have missed that before.

She loved him. She had to. She wouldn't give herself in this way if she didn't. He recognized that much about the woman that she was. The woman she'd always been.

He abandoned the fruit—it no longer held his interest when he had the sweetness of Ainsley spread out, eager and waiting before him. He quickly shucked off the rest of their clothing—noting that a bra wasn't the only undergarment she'd gone without tonight. Later he'd have to tell her just how sexy he thought that really was. But for now he was too caught up in the experience of touching her, tasting her and holding her to make the sentiment coherent.

They rolled together on the blanket, jostling and fighting, not for position but for the chance to get a bigger piece of each other. She let out a sudden gasp but he wasn't certain the cause, at least not until he rolled over onto the spreading cold of her spilled wine.

He could feel it coating his skin, mixing with the moisture from their exertion and leaving him rather sticky. She felt the same way to him as he let his hands run across her body.

He leaned up to take a sip of her skin. The heady scent of sex only enhanced the flavor of the wine. He couldn't get enough of her. Greedy, his lips strained to touch everywhere he could reach. And when that wasn't enough, he rolled her onto her stomach so he could get more.

Looming over her, he enjoyed her gasp of surprise, the way the moonlight shone across her skin and the wanton angle of her sprawled legs. He licked his way down her spine, enjoying the roll of his tongue over each vertebra. The wine was excellent—he'd made sure of that—but the taste of her was better than anything he'd ever experienced. Sweet, tart, tangy…tempting.

Ainsley rose up on her elbows, throwing a saucy smile at him over her shoulder. His cock throbbed, wanting to be inside her. Grasping her thighs, he spread her wide. Her sex glistened, wet with wanting him.

And he couldn't stop himself from taking what he knew was already his.

He quickly sheathed himself before sliding home.

Rearing back into him, she took every last inch that he had to give. They could be greedy together. Her sex pulsed around him, stealing his breath and his sanity. She was perfect, tight and warm and wet.

She moved beneath him, a sigh of pleasure leaking from her lips when she pulled him deeper. The base of his skull throbbed with the urging to just let go. Not yet. He wasn't ready for this to be over.

Their sticky skin collided again and again as he slowly thrust in and out, building, prolonging, torturing them both. Ainsley let out little pants as she met him stroke for stroke, each time pushing harder and faster against him. He didn't have to see her face to know that she was in ecstasy. He was right there with her.

He could feel her body begin to quake, the small tremors making him want to explode. *Wait, wait, just a little longer,* he told himself, knowing that the prolonged agony would be worth every second when the feel of her erupting around him finally sucked him home.

And he wasn't wrong. The wave of her release washed through him, pulsing around him and clenching him. An echoing burst of sensation started at the base of his spine, traveling down through the tip of his cock.

Heat rushed through him, radiating out of every extremity…and straight into her. Letting go, he threw back his head and surrendered to the bliss.

It was several minutes before he was coherent again. Before he registered Ainsley's body spread beneath him. Her arms and legs were thrown wide at awkward angles, but he and she were still tucked close, chest to back. The comforting pant of her breath tickled the skin of his arm.

He moved to take his weight from her but her grunt of protest stopped him. He settled for slipping down onto the blanket beside her, keeping their bodies flush against each other.

Several moments later she rolled onto her side, gathering her limbs and curling into him. Her head rested on his outstretched biceps and a smile of satisfaction gently curved her lips.

Her eyes were closed even though he knew she was awake. She looked like an angel, her hair rumpled and floating softly around her face. She was radiant and beautiful. And he wanted her with him always.

Ask her now. Do it.

Without his brain fully functioning, he reached out, running his fingers down the slope of her cheek. Her skin was so soft. Comforting.

"Come to Atlanta with me."

The reaction he got wasn't nearly what he'd expected.

Or wanted.

14

SHE JERKED OUT FROM UNDER him, scrambling to pick up the pieces of her clothing. She didn't actually put them on, just hugged them to her body as she turned to face him.

Her mind was racing.

The tattoo of her heart skipped several beats even as it urged her on to just say yes.

But she didn't.

Instead, uncontrollable fear crashed over her. Fear that if she turned her life upside down for this man, he'd turn around and leave her. Again.

He hadn't given her any assurances. He hadn't promised her forever, next week or even next month. He'd simply asked her to come with him, to leave behind everything she was and everything she had. For him.

If he'd asked her eight years ago she would have gone without hesitation. Now, she was cautious.

It was a risk she wasn't sure she was ready to take. Not based on a few weeks together.

Looking down at him she said, "I don't know, Luke."

He stood up beside her, moving to touch her even as she sidestepped out of his reach.

"Why? Surely you can do whatever you want in Atlanta."

"Probably, but I'm not sure it's the best choice for me. What is this, Luke? Are we just a fling or is this something more? It makes a difference if I'm going to uproot my entire life."

Anger flitted across his face before he controlled it. What right did he have to be angry in all this?

"I don't know what this is…. Do you? You're uprooting your life already, Ainsley. I'm just asking that you transplant somewhere close to me."

"Close to you or with you? Are you asking me to move in? Are you offering me a home or do you just want to keep me handy so you can screw me whenever you get a little stressed?"

"That's hardly fair."

"Fair? I have plans, Luke. Did you know that I got accepted to the Auburn agricultural program? I want to spend my life working on a farm, in the dirt, in the open air. I can't do that in Atlanta."

His jaw went lax as he stared at her for several seconds. His voice was quiet when he answered, "No. I didn't even realize you'd applied anywhere."

"No, you didn't. You haven't asked me what I wanted to do with my life…at least not without the focus of your question being whether my answer would mess up *your* plans. You expect me to rearrange everything for you and yet you won't make any sacrifices. You won't offer me promises." She could feel the tears clogging the back of her throat, a mixture of pain, sadness and downright anger that was a lethal combination for her composure. "You won't share any part of your life with me. What's going on with your company, what's going on in your head… You keep it all to yourself. And yet you expect me to split myself wide-open and risk it all."

She stared into his eyes, hoping for something, searching for something that just wasn't there. The center of her chest began to ache, a burning sensation that felt as if she were being ripped in two.

"I can't do it, Luke. I'm older and wiser and I've been hurt one too many times to risk it."

She turned her back on him, taking a few blind steps away, hoping that she could get beyond his sight before completely breaking down.

But he stopped her. His hands wrapped around the curve of her biceps, pulling her tight against his chest. She could feel the rise and fall of his haggard breaths. Part of her appreciated the single sign that this was as difficult for him on some level as it was for her.

His skin, still covered with wine and crushed fruit, stuck to her own. Her body wanted her to relent; even now amidst the emotional turmoil she could feel the faint buzz of sexual awareness coursing through her veins.

He dipped his head to her, his lips brushing against the curve of her neck as he whispered, "I can't offer you promises, Ainsley. You better than anyone should understand that there just aren't any. All I can tell you right now is that I want you with me."

The tears finally slipped free. She'd have given anything to hear those exact words before. Now she wanted more. She needed more. She deserved more. She wasn't a young, naive girl any longer. She was a strong, independent, intelligent woman who finally understood her own worth.

"This time, that isn't good enough."

LUKE TOSSED AND TURNED all night, rehashing his conversation with Ainsley, trying to find some way it could have turned out differently. He was a master negotiator. He'd spent years arguing his way into contracts with companies that hadn't known they needed him until he'd pointed it out.

When he'd needed those skills most, they had deserted him.

His head pounded, he couldn't sleep and his mind was restless. He wasn't happy. But he also knew that she was asking too much. He couldn't offer her promises. He couldn't guarantee her forever. It would be false advertising, something he'd tried hard over the years to avoid.

Today, for a change, he would be the first one up. He dragged his tired body out of bed, threw on jeans and a T-shirt, and made his way to the kitchen. He definitely needed caffeine in order to function today. The house was quiet, peaceful, in the minutes just after sunrise. The hustle and bustle would begin any minute, but right now…

the air was cool, the world was calm. Unfortunately, his head was still spinning.

He made a pot of coffee and settled in, but seconds after his first sip, an email pinged into the in-box on his BlackBerry. He saw immediately that it was from the orchard's client. Luke had sent them a request for the paperwork, explaining that their delay was holding up the sale.

They'd responded. With a message that said it had been completed and mailed over a week and a half ago.

At first Luke just stared down at the small screen in his palm. How could that be?

But then his brain began to spin. All the problems. All the delays. He'd been chalking them up to coincidence, timing issues and the normal delays in trying to move a sale of this magnitude through the system quickly. There were bound to be some miscues and dropped calls.

Somewhere deep inside, though, he'd wondered. Could all the mistakes really have been unintentional?

Ainsley was the one who handled the orchard's correspondence. How many times had he watched her head down the long drive to retrieve the mail? His grandmother certainly couldn't make that long walk. At least he didn't think so.

He went to Ainsley's office, deciding there was one simple way to find out the truth. Sifting through the piles of papers on her desk, it didn't take him long to find the envelope he was looking for buried beneath days and days of credit card offers and supply catalogs. Opened.

How could she have done this?

He knew she was unhappy with his decision to sell the farm, but she'd seemed resigned. Hell, she even had a plan for her life after it all went through.

So why? That's what he wanted to know. Why had Ainsley been sabotaging everything he'd been working toward?

Plunking down into the single seat in the office, Luke stared out the window. If he was honest with himself, he'd admit that over the past few days he'd begun to wonder if the delays were really coincidences. But he hadn't wanted to think Ainsley had been capable of that kind of deceit.

Not the woman who'd shared his bed, not the girl he'd once loved, not the strong and capable person she'd become. The Ainsley he knew couldn't have done something like this.

But the proof was sitting, crumpled in his hand.

Galvanized by anger, fueled by resentment and disbelief, Luke carefully slipped the letter back into the stack. He'd wait until she came down and confront her with evidence she couldn't dispute.

FOR THE FIRST TIME IN WEEKS they'd slept in separate rooms. Ainsley had jumped into the pond to wash off the sticky residue on her skin and to hide the tears that she couldn't seem to stop.

When she resurfaced Luke was gone, along with all evidence of the surprise he'd planned for her. Everything except the four-wheeler that waited silently for her return.

The next morning she sluggishly crept down the stairs an hour or so after dawn. Later than normal but she supposed no one would blame her this once. The entire farm must have known what Luke planned. How could they have missed his elaborate preparations waiting there for her? She wanted to avoid the orchard for that very reason. She didn't think she could take the knowing stares and sly winks. Not this morning.

Instead, she slipped into the office, closing her eyes as she soaked up the sunshine before putting her head down and concentrating on paying bills.

It wouldn't be long before this chore was no longer hers.

And that was precisely where he found her several hours later, her eyes bleary from lack of sleep and staring at the marching line of black numbers. She could hear him coming from halfway down the hall. His staccato steps were quick and angry. She hoped he didn't want to rehash last night. She just wasn't up for that this morning.

She was afraid that at the slightest push from him she'd fold. And that eventually they'd both regret it. She'd lain awake for hours last night going over and over her decision. It had been the right one.

So why did it hurt so much?

Whatever she'd expected, it wasn't the storm of angry man that blew into her office.

"What the hell do you think you're doing?"

"What do you mean? I'm balancing the accounts." She pointed calmly to the open ledger in front of her, knowing that in the face of such seething rage it was her best hope to come out unscathed. It had been a long time since she'd had to deal with a man this angry—since she'd moved out of her father's house—but old habits died hard and she immediately went into conciliatory mode.

However, Luke wasn't her father and she had no real fear of physical or emotional abuse at his hands. She simply didn't have the energy to deal with the kind of eruption she could see coming.

Not from him. Not today.

"Admit it. You've done everything in your power to stall the sale of the orchard." He stalked around the side of her desk, invading her space and forcing her to stand to meet him toe-to-toe.

Where was this coming from? "I've done no such thing. I've done everything you asked me to do. Hell, I even stepped in and showed the buyer around the orchard when you forgot about the scheduled meeting. I've bent over backward to help you."

"But you don't think I should sell."

"No. I don't. I've been open with you about that. But that doesn't mean I've sabotaged you."

"That's exactly what you've done. Saying you emailed the financial documents to the broker when you never did. Conveniently forgetting to give me phone messages from the Realtor. Changing appointment times without bothering to let me know. Hiding the approval documents from the client. I think that's the worst."

What the hell was he talking about? She hadn't done any of those things.

"I put the financial paperwork on the kitchen counter with yours. You never gave me the broker's email address...I couldn't email her." Ainsley made sure that her words were precise and clear, needing them to sink through the red haze surrounding Luke. "I haven't seen the paperwork from the client."

He began rummaging in the papers piled on her desk. Flipping through a stack of junk mail that she really needed to take the time to go through. But it was such a pain, a never-ending task she'd been too preoccupied to deal with for the past few weeks. Too preoccupied with him.

"Oh, really," he said, holding up an envelope from the stack. She didn't appreciate the sarcasm dripping from his words but couldn't do anything about it. She recognized the high-quality stationery that he held in his hand. Definitely from their client. But she hadn't put the letter there. She'd never seen it.

"What would you call this? I got an email from them this morning. They said they'd mailed the documents a week and a half ago. You've had this for at least a week. When were you going to tell me, Ainsley? How long were you going to let me sit here and wait?"

Disbelief and a definite feeling of dread began to churn in the pit of her stomach. "Luke, I don't know where that came from but I haven't seen it before today. Until now."

She could tell by the expression on his face that he didn't believe her. The fact that he could doubt her word hurt, but she had no intention of letting him know just how much. Yes, she might disagree with his decision, but she never would have stooped to underhanded tricks to push him into what she wanted. What she thought was right.

"Why? That's what I really want to know, Ainsley. Why would you do this? Wasn't it enough that you took Logan and Alex from me? Was it just too hard for you to let go of the home and family you stole from me? This isn't yours. Collier Orchards will never be yours."

She honestly thought she'd cried all of her tears last night. She'd felt washed up and bone-dry when she'd woken up this morning. But his words, harsh and lethal, brought more to the surface again.

She refused to let them fall. She held them back just at the edges of her control and her eyelashes. Her voice was weak and husky when she responded.

"I didn't take anything from you, Luke. You threw it away. With both hands. You walked away from me, from Logan, from your grandparents, from this place. And yes, you walked away from your son. You might not have known but you never even considered the possibility. It didn't matter to you. The life we had together, the love we shared didn't matter. At least not more than your freedom.

"I didn't try to take that away from you then and I certainly haven't tried to take it away from you now. Believe what you want, but I didn't do any of the things that you've just accused me of. Why would I? Even if you stayed, I'm leaving. I can't live here anymore. Not with you."

Without waiting for his response, she pushed past him, tearing down the hallway, knocking into the door frame of the kitchen before finally finding her way outside.

GRAN WATCHED AINSLEY run past. Shooting from her chair she was at the door in record time, especially for her. Luke's footsteps sounded behind her. She turned to look.

"What's going on? What's happened to Ainsley?"

The expression on his face mirrored the bone-deep betrayal and pain that had been stamped all over the dear child's.

When he didn't answer her, instead simply standing in the center of the hallway and staring at the closed door Ainsley had disappeared behind, she asked again, "What's wrong?"

She hated to see either of them—both of them—in this much pain.

He finally looked down at her, shaking away the emotions on his face as he did. In their place was a blank mask, nothing of the boy he'd been or the man she was so proud of.

"Nothing, Gran. A misunderstanding. I have to leave for a few days. The paperwork's finally in but the closing won't be until Friday. I'm going to take a few days at the office but I'll be back."

Gran nodded. Disappointment bubbled up inside. She would be sad to leave this place but she'd done what she could. In the end, it would either work out or it wouldn't.

Luke looked across at her, his eyes blank as he asked, "Let Ainsley know?"

"You aren't going to tell her yourself?"

Again, he glanced at the door, the turmoil returning to his face for the briefest moment. "No."

He was packed and out the door within thirty minutes. The drive home to Atlanta was a blur. Before he realized it, he was standing in the middle of the living room in his high-rise penthouse. He didn't even remember the trip.

He hadn't bothered to flip on the lights as he'd come in the door. Instead, he stood in darkness, surrounded by the gloom of dusk and his stark chrome-and-glass furniture. Until this very moment he hadn't realized how sterile and impersonal his decor was. He hadn't cared.

He'd hired a decorator; his only stipulation was that nothing resembling country could enter through the front doors. Ironically, he was sorely missing the warmth of the farm's kitchen, the well-worn boards of the hardwood floors and the scent of Ainsley as she curled next to him in the old-fashioned sleigh bed.

He stalked over to the sofa, leaving his suitcase unpacked by the door, and slumped onto the uncomfortable surface.

It took less than five minutes staring out the blank windows before he was consumed with nervous energy.

A run. He'd go for a run.

As his legs pumped beneath him eating up the pavement of the track around the park, his mind raced over his argument with Ainsley. He played her words over again and again in his mind. And paired them with the hurt and bewildered expression on her face.

She certainly hadn't appeared like someone who'd been caught in a deception.

If he was honest, he'd admit that he'd already been angry with her, upset at the way she'd simply dismissed his offer out of hand the night before. He'd been hurt that she hadn't at least thought longer about what he was offering her—a second chance for their relationship.

Was she right, though? Did he really expect her to make all the sacrifices? Or was he simply being practical? He was the one with an established career, with a company that employed hundreds of people who depended on him for their livelihood.

He was willing to sacrifice. Wasn't he?

His feet pounded in time with the churning of his brain as he attempted to think of one sacrifice that he'd made—back then or now—for their relationship.

He couldn't come up with a single example.

He couldn't even come up with one he'd made for another relationship. He'd had girlfriends in the past eight years. None more important than his work or his company. They'd all fizzled, something that hadn't bothered him. By the time the relationships were over he was finished with them, as well. He hadn't felt this urge to hang on to anything or anyone ever before.

He pushed his body until his lungs strained with the effort. The one thought running through his brain was that he'd rather be at home.

With Ainsley.

15

"GRAN, HE'S BACK."

This time Ainsley didn't need to see the trail of dust coming down the driveway; the loud hum of his car warned her.

"Of course he is, dear. He said he would be."

It had been three days since their fight. Three days since she'd seen or heard from him. Three days since he'd left without another word between them.

It was proof positive that she'd made the right decision in refusing his offer to come to Atlanta.

And she had no desire to see him now. No desire and no reason. Getting up from the table, she left the breakfast dishes sitting where they were and slipped out the back door. They rarely had reason to use it, but today she'd found one.

He'd be here long enough to drop off his overnight bag—because that's all he'd need for this stay—before heading back into town to sign the sale papers. It should be easy enough to avoid him for the next twenty-four hours.

She'd already begun packing her things; most of what she had left was odds and ends.

Luke had hired movers who would be here in the next week to box and ship everything of Gran's to Atlanta. She'd helped Gran pack what she'd need until her things arrived. Tonight would be their last night in the old house. Tomorrow they'd all be leaving, going their separate ways.

And if the thought of that made her heart ache enough to have her pressing her palm to her chest, at least she knew she'd be able to make a fresh start.

She'd be able to leave all of this behind, the memories, the sadness and the pain. She'd never forget Alex, Logan and Pops—they'd always be with her, in her heart and mind.

She found herself in front of Alex's grave. She supposed it was inevitable that one of the final places she'd want to visit was here.

She folded her limbs beneath her and collapsed onto the soft grass covering her son's grave. With a hand pressed to the sun-warmed granite, she began talking to him. It wasn't something she did often, as she'd never really had the chance to speak to him in person, to build that kind of relationship between them. It felt sort of like the one-sided conversations they'd had when she'd carried him inside her body.

"I think leaving you is the hardest. Somehow, having you close all these years helped. At least I think it did."

She patted the stone as if she were patting her son's head. "Don't blame your daddy, though, Alex. He just… He has reasons for what he does even if we don't always understand."

Over the past few days she'd thought long and hard about what had happened between them, then and now. It had taken her a while to really understand that Luke's inability to keep this place, his inability to share himself or commit to her was a result of fear. Fear of losing someone else. Better not to let them matter.

It made her sad to think of how lonely he'd be. "I worry about him. One day he's going to wake up alone and realize it's too late."

It had taken her just as long to understand that she couldn't change him. Or the circumstances. It sucked that she'd fallen in love with a man who refused to open himself up to anyone. But somewhere during one long and lonely night she'd decided that he was the one missing out. On her and on life.

But she couldn't make him embrace life, or her, if he didn't want to.

She could only control her own actions.

"Keep an eye on him for me, my beautiful baby boy."

LUKE STOPPED. HE COULD see Ainsley's head just above the rise of the hill. He moved closer, using the trees as cover. He didn't want to disturb her but he was also drawn to her presence, as if by some magnetic force he couldn't avoid.

He should have known she'd be here.

Her soft words were flung back to him on the wind. "I worry about him…"

He listened as she asked their son to watch over and protect him. Part of him wanted to go to her, to gather her in his arms and promise her that everything would be okay.

As he watched she pushed up from the ground and brushed off the seat of her shorts. She placed a kiss to her palm and pressed it to the top of the headstone. Then she turned around and walked away.

She headed in the opposite direction from where he stood, out toward the orchard and the workers picking there. He'd come up from the house, driven by the need to say his last goodbye to his parents, brother, grandfather and the son he'd never met.

Unlike Ainsley, he had no idea what to say. Instead, he stopped a few moments by each grave, simply placing his hand on the stone and remembering. By the time he walked away, his mind was filled with childhood moments he'd shared with his brother and a smile was on his face. A piece of comfort he hadn't expected today.

He returned to the house, walking into the kitchen to find his grandmother sitting at the table, her favorite mug cradled in her hands.

He hadn't done more than kiss her cheek and tell her hello when he'd walked in a little while ago. Now she looked up at him, her eyes bright and full of life like he hadn't seen them in weeks.

"Sit down."

The words were definitely a command from the sergeant who'd run most of his life. He sat.

"Ainsley finally told me what you two fought about on that last day. I want you to know that she wasn't the one who did all those things. I was."

"I know." Luke looked across at his grandmother, at the fierce purpose that glowed in her eyes, a purpose that had been missing for longer than he probably knew. It had taken him a little while to figure out what had happened. Once he'd admitted to himself that he really believed Ainsley and began searching for a different answer, it hadn't taken him long.

Gran was the only other person with access to everything she'd needed to sabotage the sale. The fact that he hadn't thought she had the capacity to devise such a plan and carry it out was his fault. He'd underestimated her, something he should have known better than to do.

"I did it. I tore up your phone messages, threw away Ainsley's paperwork, changed the broker's appointment and hid the letter in the pile of junk mail. I did those things. Ainsley doesn't have a devious bone in her body and if you don't already know that then you're a bigger imbecile than I thought."

It was the longest speech he'd heard from his grandmother in over eight years. He'd gotten used to her simple sentence answers and single-word requests. At the moment part of him wished that frail woman back.

"Why? If you didn't want to leave that much you should have said something."

"Like that would have made a difference. But this has

nothing to do with leaving the orchard. Your grandfather and I knew that was a likelihood if he gave the orchard to you. You think he would have made that kind of decision without talking to me about it? This was about you and Ainsley."

That puzzled him. He'd expected to hear her say something about not wanting to leave the home she'd known for most of her life. "How was sabotaging the sale of the orchard for me and Ainsley?"

"You belong together. At least I thought you did until three days ago. But it looks like I was wrong." She raised her eyes, filled with sadness and disappointment, to his. "The two of you just can't seem to get things right. I'm all for fighting for what you want but love shouldn't be that difficult. It should be something that fills your soul not causes the kind of pain I saw you both going through."

He should probably be angry. Part of him was, but not enough to do anything about what she was saying. "You did all this to meddle in my love life?"

She shrugged. Honest to God, shrugged and said, "I was wrong."

For that he really did want to stomp around and shout at her. But he also wanted to lean over and smack a kiss to her cheek. No matter what he'd done, as a boy, teenager, or headstrong man, she'd been there for him and loved him. Unconditionally. And she'd always welcomed him home with open arms and not a single word of recrimination.

That was the kind of acceptance you just couldn't find everywhere.

She shuffled over to him, laying her palm across the ridge of his cheek. "You do what you need to, Luke. Whatever you decide is fine with me."

Gran left him alone, standing in the heart of the house that he'd grown up in. The quiet pressed in against his chest and suddenly what he wanted more than anything was to get out.

Snatching the keys from the counter, he headed to the drive, dropped into the waiting leather seat and pushed his Jag to the limits of its motor as he raced into town.

He arrived for the closing early, but it didn't seem to matter. The lawyer, his Realtor and the Kincaids all arrived within five minutes of him. They were as eager as he was to get this over with.

They all took their seats around the flashy boardroom table in the conference room at the lawyer's office. A stack of papers sat in front of him, waiting for his signature.

He'd been through this before. Well, not this precise moment but many like it. Ready to sign his life away on the dotted line so to speak. He signed off on multimillion-dollar contracts every week. This was nothing.

So why did his pen hover above the page, refusing to move any closer?

He stared down at the black letters on the crisp white page as the lawyer droned in his ear about what they meant. He didn't actually hear the words, just the slow, smooth cadence of the man's voice as he detailed what went into selling his childhood home.

Never in a million years did Luke expect to be sitting

here, palms sweating, a weight centered in the middle of his chest, unable to actually sign the damn things.

Visions flashed through his mind, his brother, his grandfather, even a memory he'd forgotten until that very moment. A trip that he and Logan had taken to visit Gran and Pops with their parents after they'd just turned three.

He remembered the smile on his mother's face as she linked arms with his father and walked down the path beneath the trees. He and Logan had skipped ahead, playing hide-and-seek between the trunks.

Was it a real memory or one his subconscious had just made up? Did it matter?

He could see his family there, happy. He could see Ainsley there, the first time he'd noticed her, running through the trees in the moonlight. The way she'd looked this afternoon, her hand pressed to the top of Alex's grave.

"Mr. Collier?"

The lawyer leaned across the table, placing his hand against the sleeve of Luke's suit. He'd worn it today because he felt comfortable in it. It was what he was used to. But while he'd been at the farm, he'd gotten used to other things. Like having Ainsley in his life. Like the slower pace of farm living.

Like the happiness he'd found here with her.

He'd been back in Atlanta for three days. Three miserable and lonely days. He'd finally come to an agreement with Miyazaki, a better deal than he'd expected, actually.

He'd been very pleased. And the first person he'd wanted to tell was Ainsley. Ainsley, who wasn't there.

At first he'd been angry. Angry with her and with himself. She'd turned him down without even considering what moving to Atlanta could mean for them. But she'd been right. Not once had he considered her plans before he'd made the request.

How could he become so addicted to someone in such a short amount of time? He honestly couldn't envision his life without Ainsley in it. Fighting with her. Loving her. Sharing his days with her. When he looked at his future she was there. She always had been.

The one woman he couldn't live without no matter how hard he'd tried.

He couldn't do it. He simply couldn't sign the papers and give it all up.

Ainsley and the orchard were tied together so tightly he couldn't have one without the other. And he knew, without a shadow of a doubt, that he wanted Ainsley. And if that meant keeping this place for her, then that's what he'd do.

Looking across the table to the couple waiting there, he set down his pen and apologized. "I'm sorry. I don't think I can sell after all."

Mrs. Kincaid looked flabbergasted. Mr. Kincaid just looked angry. Luke quickly headed off the argument he could see coming.

"I'll be happy to double your earnest money. And if we ever do decide to sell I'll give you first right of refusal."

Pushing away from the table, Luke signaled the end to the conversation. It was his decision to make and he'd made it.

"If you'll excuse me, there's a woman I need to go find."

AINSLEY LIFTED A SUITCASE into the trunk of her car. It was the same beat-up Civic she'd had for ten years now. She hardly ever drove it…hardly had a reason to. Tomorrow she'd drive away from this place for good. She hoped she would never look back but realized it was probably too much to expect.

There were a couple of boxes and another suitcase sitting by the far left tire, waiting their turn to be loaded.

She reached for the second suitcase, but slowed halfway there. Bent as she was, she could see straight down the driveway. This time, she saw the tail of dust before she heard the racing engine that signaled Luke's return.

Clenching her teeth tight together, she purposely turned her head so she could no longer watch his approach and continued putting everything she owned into the trunk.

His tires spun on the gravel as he skidded to a stop several feet away. The sharp ping and protesting sound of the small stones being thrown made her frown. What was wrong with him?

The car door slammed with enough force to make her cringe.

She ignored that, too.

He walked over to her, the sound of his feet heavy

on the ground between them. She could see the tips of his shoes, polished and perfect. She'd bet they were real handmade leather and cost more than all of her possessions combined.

"What are you doing?"

She bent for the last box, looking up at him from her prone position as she tried to get a good grip on the uncooperative surface. The box was big and unwieldy and if they'd been in a happier place she would have asked him to lift it for her.

"I'd think that was obvious. I'm packing."

"Why?"

What did he mean, why? "Because I'm leaving." She said the words slowly, as if to a child who couldn't seem to grasp the simplest of concepts.

"No, you're not."

With an exasperated sigh, she finally straightened with the box balanced in her hands. He reached for it, trying to snatch it from her. They fought. She lost. And the box ended up on its side in the dirt at her feet, the contents spilling around them both.

She turned on him. Angry for what he was doing. Angry that he'd signed the damn papers. Angry that he wasn't the man she wanted him to be.

"What the hell is wrong with you?" She lashed out at him, pushing the flat of her hands squarely into the center of his chest and shoving. He rocked back on his heels for a nanosecond before recovering. Which was so frustrating. She wanted to hurt him in some way and she couldn't even manage to do that.

She tried again, putting every last ounce of her strength into the attack. But instead of fighting her or moving with the force, he grasped her wrists, held her hands flat to his chest and pulled her in close to his body.

She struggled against him. "Let me go!"

Instead he crushed his mouth to hers in a punishing kiss. She wanted to fight—to deny that he could make her feel anything—but it was a battle she could not win. It took seconds for her body to betray her, melting against him in immediate surrender to anything he wanted, everything she could give.

He devoured her, his arms imprisoning her body, his entire being looming over and surrounding her. And she more than let him, she fully engaged, showing him the strength of her own desire.

When he finally pulled back, it was only to give her enough room to suck in a much-needed breath. A breath she used to whisper, "Damn you."

He gathered her close again. This time instead of assaulting her senses, he tucked her tight against him. Her cheek was buried in the curve of his neck, his chin resting lightly on the crown of her head.

"I didn't sell."

"You what?"

"I couldn't sign the papers."

She pushed against his chest, wanting to look at him, to see into his eyes. But he wouldn't let her, refusing to loosen his embrace. She wasn't sure if that was because he didn't want her to see him or because he needed to hold on to her so desperately.

As desperately as she suddenly needed to hold on to him.

"I sat there, with a pen in my hand ready to go and I physically couldn't do it. I started to remember everything, the laughter, the years, even the fights that I had with Pops."

He was silent a moment before he continued.

"I even remembered my parents here. A memory I didn't know I had. I barely knew them, Ainsley. I can't remember anything about them. But I remember them here."

She could hear the bewilderment and pain in his voice. He'd lost his parents so young, never really knowing what he'd lived without. Until today. Today he'd remembered what he'd lost, possibly for the first time in his life.

She wanted to soothe the pain away, to protect him from it any way that she could. Her hands stirred within his hold, silently asking for release. He didn't give it. She wasn't even sure he was aware of how tight he was holding her.

"But you know what was the worst? I had a clear vision in my head of how our life could have been here. Kids running down the path in front of us as we walked hand in hand through the trees. And I wanted that. I wanted it more than anything else I've ever wanted in my life."

His words were seductive, the future she'd always dreamed of with him. But she was afraid to let the hope blossom in her chest again. Afraid, because that had never been what he'd wanted before today.

She voiced her doubts with a whisper that melted into the warmth of his chest, "Even your success? Even your freedom?"

This time he did let her pull away, looking down at her with a light in his eyes that she had never seen.

"Absolutely. I've been lonely for the past eight years and I never realized it. Not until I had you back in my life and walked away from you. Again. I was gone three days, Ainsley, but it felt like three years.

"I have everything I've ever wanted. And it doesn't mean anything to me if I don't have you to share it with."

Her head was spinning. He'd just said everything to her that she'd ever wanted to hear. And more, actually. But she didn't know what any of it meant.

"What are you saying?"

He leaned close, pressing his forehead to hers. She could feel the heat of his skin sinking into her own and the brush of his breath against her cheeks. His eyes stared straight into hers and she saw it there before he ever said a word.

"I'm saying I love you, Ainsley. And I can't live my life without you."

Her knees buckled. One minute they were there and the next it was as if they were dust. She sagged into him, his hold on her the only thing keeping her from hitting the gravel at their feet.

Sweeping her up into his arms, he carried her onto the worn wooden porch, to a faded rocker tucked into a shady corner. The warm summer sun didn't reach here, but she wasn't cold. In fact, hope and heat coursed through her in equal measures making her heart beat faster than it ever had before.

He pressed a cool kiss to her lips, a quick check of her status more than an expression of passion. "Are you okay?"

She nodded, unable to voice any one thought. There were so many racing around in her head she wasn't sure where to start.

"I'll do whatever you want," he said, "I'll sell the company. We can live here and farm peaches until we're old and gray and can't get off of this porch. I want what my grandparents had and I want it with you."

His words finally galvanized her. "I don't want you to sell your business, Luke. I never have. I wouldn't ask you to give that up any more than I'd ask you to change the color of your eyes. It's part of who you are. Part of the man I love."

His green eyes flared and she realized that even though she'd known for weeks that she still loved him, it was the first time she'd actually said the words aloud. She'd held them so close to her heart that she somehow thought he already knew.

"We'll make it work." This time she was the one to reach up and place a kiss on his waiting mouth. She filled the connection with every speck of her hope and happiness.

He'd offered to give up everything he held dear for her. It was more sacrifice than she needed but the gesture certainly cemented his willingness to place her first in his life. That was all the promise she needed. They'd figure out the rest as they went along.

Their hands and mouths wandered, her sharp breaths turning into quick gasps in a matter of moments. And as much as it felt as if they were alone in the world cocooned together on the front porch, they were actually surrounded by people.

"Luke."

"Hmm," was his response, coupled by a groan of surrender as his hands pushed up her shirt to find the waiting peak of her breast.

"Probably not the best place."

Even as he pulled away from her, staring down with unfocused and heat-glazed eyes, she could hear Gran shuffling around in the kitchen just on the other side of the wall.

Apparently he could, too, because the glitter slowly faded, once again turning tender. A smile curled the corners of his lips and crinkled the edges of his eyes.

"I don't think I'll ever be able to thank you."

"For what?"

"For taking care of my family when I wouldn't. For protecting this place when I couldn't. For saving it all for me even though I didn't want you to. For doing what was right for me whether I realized it or not."

Happy tears formed at the corners of her eyes. She smiled through them. "Even when I wanted to hate you, I stayed here for you. Hoping you'd come home. Hoping you'd come back."

Epilogue

LUKE STUMBLED OUT ONTO the porch, the bright stab of sunshine shooting straight through his skull.

"You look like hell."

He turned to look at his wife, sitting quietly in the rocker in the dimmest and coolest part of the porch. Even through his jet-lagged, sleep-deprived haze he could see that she was beautiful. Earthy and ethereal all at the same time. She was right where she belonged, sitting on the front porch of this hundred-year-old house, acres of peach trees at her back.

She rocked back and forth with a serene motion, a small smile playing at her lips. But it was the hint of devilment in her eyes that had him taking quick steps toward her.

Japan might only be a flight away, but it was a hell of a long flight and two weeks was way too damn long to be gone. He'd missed his wife. But Miyazaki was satisfied and he'd cemented another five-year exclusive contract with the company. He hoped it was that long before he had to fly back.

The trips away from the farm were getting harder and harder. He didn't like being away from Ainsley. But he was home now....

Just as he was about to reach for her, to pull her into the heat that was suffusing him from his toes to his skull, a tiny arm popped out between them and gave a slow, languorous wave.

The motion startled him into stopping.

"I thought she was asleep." It had been way too quiet for their six-week-old daughter not to be. She was a hellcat, that little one. Definitely a fighter. And already he knew she had him wrapped around her little finger.

"She practically is." Shuffling the mound of baby and blankets around in her lap, Ainsley managed to right all of her clothes and stand up in what looked to him like one smooth motion. He was constantly awed by the effortless way she'd taken to motherhood.

He'd had a little harder time of it but they'd managed to get through it. Together.

Switching Rebecca to her shoulder, Ainsley wrapped her free arm around him and brought him close. Her lips were sweet, sweeter than the fruit that was just starting to form on the trees around them. He deepened the kiss, responding to the ever-present desire that overwhelmed him whenever he touched her.

She leaned back, breaking their kiss but keeping her body tight against his.

"You got home late."

He frowned, wrinkling his nose. He didn't want to fight with her. Not today. Not now.

She just laughed, that twinkle of mischief deep in her eyes. "You can make it up to me tonight."

Before he could respond, or attempt to finagle his way into an earlier reunion, she yelled, "Logan, Daddy's up," and the smallest ball of energy he'd ever seen came bolting around the side of the house.

"Daddy, Daddy, Daddy!"

Gran shuffled slowly behind him, taking the trek from the swing set to the porch at her own pace. She had good days and bad, but Luke was convinced she was going to outlive all of them. No one could have matched Logan's enthusiasm anyway, not even him.

His son was hard to keep up with, just starting to shed the first layers of his baby fat, turning from a toddler into a little boy. In a few months he'd be starting kindergarten, a step Luke wasn't sure any of them were ready for—least of all the school.

He watched as his son raced for the stairs, taking them two at a time before launching himself into the air, certain that his father would be there to catch him. Oh, to be that young and full of faith again.

He'd certainly lost his for a while. But as he swept Logan up into the air, twirling him around, he snagged Ainsley's waist and brought his whole family along for the ride.

He'd found it again, here, in the last place he would have ever thought to look.

* * * * *

COMING NEXT MONTH

Available April 26, 2011

You can find more information on upcoming Harlequin® titles, free excerpts and more at
www.HarlequinInsideRomance.com.

REQUEST YOUR FREE BOOKS!
2 FREE NOVELS PLUS 2 FREE GIFTS!

red-hot reads!

*With an evil force hell-bent on destruction,
two enemies must unite to find a truth that turns
all-too-personal when passions collide.*

*Enjoy a sneak peek in Jenna Kernan's next installment
in her original* TRACKER *series, GHOST STALKER,
available in May, only from Harlequin Nocturne.*

"**W**ho are you?" he snarled.

Jessie lifted her chin. "Your better."

His smile was cold. "Such arrogance could only come from a Niyanoka."

She nodded. "Why are you here?"

"I don't know." He glanced about her room. "I asked the birds to take me to a healer."

"And they have done so. Is that *all* you asked?"

"No. To lead them away from my friends." His eyes fluttered and she saw them roll over white.

Jessie straightened, preparing to flee, but he roused himself and mastered the momentary weakness. His eyes snapped open, locking on her.

Her heart hammered as she inched back.

"Lead who away?" she whispered, suddenly afraid of the answer.

"The ghosts. Nagi sent them to attack me so I would bring them to her."

The wolf must be deranged because Nagi did not send ghosts to attack living creatures. He captured the evil ones after their death if they refused to walk the Way of Souls, forcing them to face judgment.

"Her? The healer you seek is also female?"

"Michaela. She's Niyanoka, like you. The last Seer of Souls and Nagi wants her dead."

Jessie fell back to her seat on the carpet as the possibility of this ricocheted in her brain. Could it be true?

"Why should I believe you?" But she knew why. His black aura, the part that said he had been touched by death. Only a ghost could do that. But it made no sense.

Why would Nagi hunt one of her people and why would a Skinwalker want to protect her? She had been trained from birth to hate the Skinwalkers, to consider them a threat.

His intent blue eyes pinned her. Jessie felt her mouth go dry as she considered the impossible. Could the trickster be speaking the truth? Great Mystery, what evil was this?

She stared in astonishment. There was only one way to find her answers. But she had never even met a Skinwalker before and so did not even know if they dreamed.

But if he dreamed, she would have her chance to learn the truth.

*Look for GHOST STALKER by Jenna Kernan,
available May only from Harlequin Nocturne,
wherever books and ebooks are sold.*

Harlequin *Desire*

ALWAYS POWERFUL, PASSIONATE AND PROVOCATIVE.

USA TODAY **BESTSELLING AUTHOR**

MAUREEN CHILD

BRINGS YOU ANOTHER PASSIONATE TALE

KINGS *of* **CALIFORNIA**

KING'S MILLION-DOLLAR SECRET

Rafe King was labeled as the King who didn't know how to love. And even he believed it. That is, until the day he met Katie Charles. The one woman who shows him taking chances in life can reap the best rewards. Even when the odds are stacked against you.

Available May, wherever books are sold.